The Troubler of Israel

BOOKS BY ANDREW MITIN

Time Spent Away
Among the Alcoves

The Troubler of Israel

ANDREW MITIN

RESOURCE *Publications* · Eugene, Oregon

THE TROUBLER OF ISRAEL

Resource Publications
An Imprint of Wipf and Stock Publishers
199 W. 8th Ave., Suite 3
Eugene, OR 97401

www.wipfandstock.com

PAPERBACK ISBN: 978-1-6667-5596-1
HARDCOVER ISBN: 978-1-6667-5597-8
EBOOK ISBN: 978-1-6667-5598-5

VERSION NUMBER 092622

THE CAST

Elijah   a prophet of Israel
Ahab   Israel's King
Jezebel   Ahab's wife, a daughter of Phoenicia
Ummashtart   a widow of Sidonia
Resheph   the widow's son

Nasir
Zacharias   Israelites
Taavi

Obadiah   Palace Administrator
Hannibal   Chief Priest
Priests   Servants of Baal
Messenger   Jezebel's servant
Chorus   Priests of Baal

1

AHAB, KING OF ISRAEL, and Queen Jezebel mourn the death of Hiel's youngest son, Segub, who has died during the reconstruction of Jericho. The King is distraught that Joshua's prophecy concerning such an event has come to pass. Even more, he is perplexed by the prophet Elijah's bold prediction of a coming draught. Despite Jezebel's doubts that Ahab is fully committed to her religion, she encourages the King that Baal will favor him.

Jezebel: My gods, have you brought me here to witness
    The weakness of these Kings of Israel?
    Day after day, from the sun's rising to
    Its fall, his hands wring to extract from air
    The forgotten blessings of Omri's reign.
    But these Kings are alike: each from others
    Have taken the crown with swords through bloodshed;
    Through ending royal lives with spears and stones
    They have established their perilous thrones.
    And will this one fare better in his rule?
    It is his firm adherence to Yahweh,
    To the ancient beliefs of his forebears,
    That Ahab deflects the glory of Baal.
    Who is this god to honored Tyrians?
    And who but to Baal do we bend our knees?
    He has no stake in these false prophesies.
    Does his wisdom deign to bother over
    Insignificant events, of rats' lives?

Who was this Joshua who proclaimed ill,
Who vowed one's firstborn for setting a stone
Upon the ruins of forgotten cities?
The blood of Abiram and of Segub
Are nothing to me and easy to give
For the reclaimed glory of Jericho,
Another jewel in Ahab's fine crown.
Look at him! Enclosed by his retinue,
A flock of advisors squawking their aims,
Estranged from one another, with their eyes
Launching spears into spleens, hoping to rise
Greater into the history of kings.
And my king amidst them, gaunt and pale-skinned.
With bloodshot eyes wobbling on puny legs,
He is led by their uproar, carried by
Dry hopes these counselors prescribe, evermore.
And am I here to lift up this crisp reed?
To squeeze water from this rock, have I come?
My Baal deal with me, be it severe,
If by year's end I've not made from this man
A roaring lion against Israel!
From my own fine house will come royal lines
Mighty to save, the deeds of whom will blot
Forever the ineptitude of these
Who call themselves King, whose robes drag through filth.
Bah! Come closer my foolish one, that I
May clearly hear your troubles and comfort
You during your baked land's irritation.
My great and Worthy King! What vexes so
Your royal airs that rush through splendid halls?

Ahab: What have I done that hasn't already been?
    Where in the annals of our great Kings are
    Their chief decisions bemoaned as mine are?
    Is not Aram to us as Philistines
    In the time of judges, when the King's voice

Was yet to be heard and his will followed?
Treaties are made and compromises kept
When the anointing oil is poured out;
When the crown is placed and the robe is draped,
Then is the chosen nation manifest.
What have I done that my fathers did not?
Show me how novel the plans I've proffered
In the archives of Israel's great Kings.
Open the history books, guide my gaze
Across the lives of my predecessors.
Did not my father Omri kill Zimri,
Who struck down defenseless Elah, drunkard,
In the home of Arza, the palace guard?
And what is the price of regicide, but
Palaces engulfed in flames, burned to ash?
Then Omri was stronger than Tibni of
Ginath, his followers unyielding.
He bought the hill of Samaria on
Which we grafted Ashera's tree, sacred.
Nadab was struck down by Baasha who was
Lifted from dust and made leader only
For city dogs and birds of the rich plain
To feed on the line of Israel's kings.
And Jeroboam, did he not erect poles
On every hill and beneath every tree
Whose branches spread blessings over the land?
It was his decree to appoint as priests
All who wanted to don those blessed robes.
And to disavow Levi's line further
He constructed two golden calves, saying:
'It is too much to worship at Temple;
Here, oh Israel, are your faithful gods!'
And the priests made sacrifice to these calves
For their Sovereign's good, for sake of the land.
And am I first to take these foreign wives
Into the temple of the Lord? Have I

Not initiated the ways of peace
For a people surrounded on all sides
By enemies who would tear us in two?
Did not Solomon, in all his wisdom,
Congest his palace with a swarm of wives,
Whose presence secured Judah's weak borders?
Still, he comes to our side, this ecstatic —
A thorn despite mourning for sons of Hiel —
To take away the rain, to stop the dew.

Jezebel: Our mighty King. Do not take so to heart
The ravings of a man in camel's hair.
Should one who's sustained on the locust swarm,
Who fought off the bee's sting for their honey
Bring your mood so low? Who is this yahweh
That his ambassador should be so styled?
Show me the merits of his followers
And I will delight by recording yours:
On the highest hill of Samaria
You built the Rain God's temple. You crafted
Its columns from the finest marble and
Ordained the design of its abacus.
The architrave, the frieze and the cornice
Are the envy of all entablatures.
Even Solomon in all his glory
Failed to match the beauty in both wealth
And in the prowess of your skilled tradesmen.
I marveled as I climbed the temple hill.
And when I had achieved the sacred steps,
When first I gazed into the inner parts,
I knew my father had not wasted my
Influence upon an inferior.
Baal's provisions kiss your crown and run down
The lithe contours of its cream cherubim.
Those hallowed images of foreign lands
Baal will convert to his ardent purpose.

How like him you are, my master and King,
When attentions are turned away from doubt
To honor her leading toward great esteem.
This fertility shrine ensures a boon.
The venerated rites of the small rooms,
Where favor awaits those who enact them,
Assure us of the love of Dagan's son.
Uncrease your brow. Why do you still frown so?
Never has holiness been so rampant;
Do elaborate ways wed so well with ease?
Everything that grows here below, praise him!
May the voices of the faithful mingle
Not with others — whose incense is most foul,
Whose vain worship and haughty leading
Will drive them into the coffers of Ahab —
But with your faithful legion, evermore.

Ahab: Most trusted advisors, your lights expose
The well-worn path that lies before us now.
I will think on your suggestions as I
Walk with my Queen. Your words are my soul's balm.
Those images are sacrilege to you;
Their soft forms poor reflections of your own.
In all my kingdom you are most honored.
I lack nothing in you who brings me good.
With wisdom you assign maiden's duties,
In knowledge you guide the spindler's fingers.
The thickest tapestries adorn our walls;
The finest satins drape our bodies and
So your good King is respected and feared
As he takes his place before the elders.
Your people call you blessed, for your charm
And beauty goes before you, marching forth,
Proclaiming surpassing nobility
To the children of disparate nations.

Jezebel: My Lord and my King, there is none like you
  To gain the favor of the gods, be they
  Of this land or the lands of your subjects.
  Even the high god Baal, the Baal Shamen,
  To whom you've taken with fervent resolve,
  Walks before you and behind. He does not
  Abide by the words of deranged mystics.
  See how lush the land is, how green the hills.
  Your storehouses are filled to great swelling;
  Your armory will clothe as many men
  As there are lowland sycamores abed;
  As many blossoms of the white storax
  So now are the vessels in your harbors
  That take your wine and your oil to the
  Gates of remote kingdoms that honor you,
  King Ahab, from whom all blessings shall flow.

Ahab: What you say is right and true, my fair Queen.
  Still, I have read the tomes, and though favors
  Be not strangers to me, curses run deeper.
  Today ruin will be my bedfellow.

Jezebel: So you've said, my King. And I have listened.
  Yet how many years since Abiram passed?
  How many nights that dear Segub has waned?
  And yet the cedar gates are vigorous,
  The foundations have been laid in hard loam.
  The walls were established through immense stones
  That none could conceive carrying alone.
  Hewn with fine chisels and muted hammers
  They are united together to make
  A single rock of stone naturally
  Existing in Israel's warm bosom.
  Can such things happen without strong leaders?
  Do marvels rise from less divine hands, or
  Fire materialize in cloudless skies?

Ahab: Peace, my sober one. Do not be so riled.
    Ancient words are weighty as sand, I know.
    And in the building of walls men are crushed.
    On the site of new nations blood must spill.
    Yet the cold tremors will not dissipate,
    The chill from bad omens does not relent.

Jezebel: Poor Elijah. How brave! He predicts drought
    In this arid land used to shower's lack.
    How inspired to proclaim at mourning!
    The funeral rites we've ably performed.
    We have fulfilled our vows, so I met you;
    I have looked for you and have found you — Come!
    Let's think of this no more, but enjoy
    Our bed of colored linens from Egypt,
    The aroma of cinnamon, of myrrh.
    Though not conducted in our bright temple,
    Such sacraments as ours will be honored
    By Almighty Baal; Goddess Asherah
    Will hear of our love and bless the land with
    Gifts from all the sons — El's blessed sons.
    If it takes all night, until the cock crows,
    The gods will know of our faithful union.

2

HAVING RECEIVED WORD FROM Yahweh, Elijah flees Segub's funeral. He races east of the Jordan to the Kerith Ravine where he is fed by ravens. He waits for Yahweh and when Elijah's prophecy comes to pass, the brooks dry up. Soon the word of the Lord comes to him, saying: *Go at once to Zarephath of Sidon and stay there. I have commanded a widow in that place to supply you with food.* Elijah makes his way.

Elijah: A little further now to man's warm light.
 From the silent address of dried brook beds
 And the mean crags of raven-fueled dawns,
 To the strength of wine-dark meats and of bread —
 To compassionate company, kin — lead.
 How many days since a rain fell upon
 The fertile land of my innocent youth?
 How many nights since the impassive moon
 Appeared in full term weighty with promise?
 Like the east star it still lights my way through
 Banana groves and arable pastures,
 Away from the King's guard, intent upon
 The head of your servant, hidden in wilds.
 I have turned my ankles on many stones;
 Briars scratch my face; they tear at my cheeks.
 My lacerated hands catch worried falls
 That bend my knees upon Your majesty.

Still, I run — for Your Word's glory, I run.
'Neither dew nor rain except at my call,'
And this for three years. Now honor my plea.
Nearer now to man's honest roar, I hear.
Israel is no land watered by springs
Nor do fit rivers irrigate its soil;
It is not as Egypt was to Your sons,
But fully dependent on the rain You send
To sustain our herds, fill our storehouses.
Woe to the land of Ahab and Hiel
Of Bethel who rebuilt Jericho's walls!
They forgot the words of Joshua who
Promised the price of such undertakings:
'By his firstborn he will lay foundations;
At the cost of joy will he set the gates.'
Should such a heritage be abandoned?
Will mere men remove history's etched stones
And remember your name no more, oh Lord?
The din from the priests of Baal finds Your ears;
To Asherah's babbling priests, retort.
How long will You watch their sexual rites?
For how long will such acts bemuse Your eyes?
They fortify their wills against Your own.
The temple reeks of debased Ketoret;
Of stacte and onycha mixed with chaff
Whose aromas mingle with prostitutes.
From these detestable practices come
Heavy yields: the rains in spring and
Healthy generations, the tongues of whom
Will never lift Your name in humble prayer.
Oh! had Ahab's ears been stopped when he heard
The Phoenician's alluring words of love.
Her proud bearing uniting with his own
Has brought upon the blest land of Jacob
Dark rivulets of bull's blood shed by priests
For the sanctification of lost souls.

By pigs is Baal appeased and from their flesh
His retinue is nourished — for a time.
Upon the altars are men's firstborn son's
Little veins opened that they may be blessed;
For a home laden with the world's riches
They leave, forever charred, remnants of love.
And in the roiling cosmos Your visage
Reflects the inscrutable moon, vacant!
Closer comes a warm light from burning fires
And a welcome place to slacken cold bones,
To forget for a time the coming times.

Nasir: Israel is parched and cracked without rain.
Now are our heels bruised upon this terrain.
Our herds lie thin and stretched upon the dust,
Our flocks whither and pass despite our fuss.
Wells pass away. There is no slake for shoots;
There are no grapes on the vine, no plump fruits.
Wine-less casks ache as ravens pick the head
Leaving no grain for the oxen to tread.
The Lord is like an enemy: bow strung,
He takes aim at the hearts of old and young.

Zacharias: Look at the cloak that once covered my girth.
Gaze now at these twigs, how the fabric hangs.
Never before have my ribs been so played?
Not even as a boy chasing spadefoots
Through rocky streams and over boulders stout
Did I imagine a physique like this.
No, in our fantasies of future selves
These ravaged forms never entered our minds.
My stomach cramps and my muscles contract;
My hands kink with slight strain; vision fails me.
I can't see the cup or grip its handle
To refresh my lips with oblivion.
Remember how we ran? We leapt and laughed

At the days to come, days of ease and joy
With our wives and sons, candlelit tables,
Soft prayers gently sung, oven hot with bread,
The Torah read by us to ours, ardent.
Its truth manifest in that humane scene.
And now —

Taavi: — now is the time for honest truth:
Before the rains ceased and vines bore fruit,
When the fields were plowed by able oxen
And refreshed from wells our forefathers dug,
You sat right here and bewailed your fate:
'Oh, that my fields resembled Asa's,
That his wife was my own betrothed, his sons
Fruit of my seed wed with a friendly womb.'
The world misbehaves today no more than
Yesterday and the same as tomorrow.
'Life was better before. The sun shone brighter
When we were young, the land more giving.'
Yet when dew rose from the ground and the rains
Strafed the earth, you could not be found except
To wet your gullet then purge forth the same.
And you are never lost to those who know
Where to find the trail, trod here to home.

Zacharias: And now my hearth is bereft of warm minds.
Gone are the ones who filled my life with hope;
Gone to the ends of the earth and further
Afield to places only the gods see.
Look upon your dogged servant, you kings
On the thrones of far-off Phoenicia!
What do I have yet that you still require?
Look upon my store and take what is yours.
My land is desiccated by your hand;
My herds are thinned worse than this feeble form.
My children were not enough for your thirst,

Our hordes of little ones did not slack
Your desire for more and more — and still more!
But every morning and in the evening
Are trumpets blown to alert your people
Of another round of fruitless feeding.
How long, oh lord, will your eyes forget me?
How long before ears catch wind of my cry?
Are my wife's favors not pleasant to you?
Her body is keen; grant time her spirit.
Strange men and priests are not her company,
Neither are palace rooms used to her wares.
Listen again to our refrains of prayer;
Look upon mine that are left with kindness.
Do not halt my storehouse with impatience.

Taavi: I forget, and maybe you can help me:
Have we sung such things in this hapless place?
Perhaps that tune was played before my time,
When my father's shadow fell with your own
Upon this dilapidated hovel?
The joys I recall have nothing to do
With crops and vines, with herds or constant wives;
But with drink and bawdy chicks loosed upon
Our senses, save that which is too common.
It is our present circumstances that
Bring precious fancies to your addled mind.
The maxim is well known: he who suffers
In this feeble body is done with sin;
And so are we who overwhelm this dump
Wanting healthy refreshment from sour ills.

Nasir: We are here today, not as like before,
To lament our wayward lives not lived for
Our own rights, but by duty to a king
Who has us prance 'round, like demons of spring,
Attached to Asherah's aberrant poles.

New laws replace those written in our scrolls
That send our wives to the devil's temple
To please high priests' urges, there dissembled
To fetch highest price for favors given;
Woe, this should befall us under heaven.

Elijah: Lord, God of Abraham and Israel,
My heart does not swerve from your decreed task.
My resolve is as strong as required
By Your word, for by Your word are men saved.
Your people suffer in due course, brought on
By generations of profligate acts
Inspired each season by last year's evils.
Each in their own way followed Jeroboam,
Whose golden calves lured from Jerusalem
The faithfulness of an errant people.
Now is the time of contest near at hand.
The presence of Baal in this land affronts
The one true God's purpose for His loved ones.
The sufferings of strained belief will reap
Attitudes of honor; deliverance
From affliction warrants a closer bond:
You will call them blessed who stand before You
And You will honor those who remember
Your kindness, renewed every morning.

Nasir: Yahweh's hand is ready to pay earned wrath;
His arm comes forward with the whistling lath.
The rivers and streams, the trickling brooks,
The dew that softens the morning, forsook.
Temple voices abandon the psalter;
The Lord has forgotten His altar.
Look, oh Lord, and consider my lament:
We have had our fill of this ill content.
Women eat their own, children they care for.
Whom have you admonished like this before

Zacharias: Remember me when I have gone away.
   When I no longer have a form to fill
   Out these rags and my voice echoes no more
   Off these hills of my childhood paradise.
   Remember that we laughed together here,
   Commiserated together here and
   It was here as men that we joined in song
   Of our lives lived fair beneath gentle suns.
   Oh, that those days were not so far away;
   That by grace, not our own, to share again
   Odes of joy for the well-wrought crop brought in.

Taavi: I was but a boy when the fields produced.
   I sojourned at my father's hip waiting
   For time fulfilled when fields, wives and livestock
   Would be mine. And for what? For withered teats
   And hard fallows my able plow can't plunge?
   But days of drought are not new, neither days
   Of sorrow; and who can predict a love
   That stays, whether of wives or deities?
   I have heard Yahweh's name whispered in tones
   Of both elegy and spite, never in praise.
   Who would celebrate one whose right hands use
   Their thrones to bring new gods into hallowed halls,
   There to burden distraught people still more
   In the bewitchment of some other ones?
   Be rid of them all! Let them torment sons
   In another land and leave us to die
   With bent backs and calloused hands in good time.

Nasir: Now friends, calm yourselves. We are all so weary?
   At odds with anxiety from worry?
   When I was a boy my father's father
   Read the Torah, he approached with honor
   Into the wisdom of his ancestors;

Of this holy word he was attester.
That word continues to speak in the breeze;
Its truth will move our hearts and hear our pleas.
A storm from the heavens is close at hand;
Godly refreshment will come to this land

Taavi: If you believe the things you say to me
What is your word concerning this drought's fury?
To what purpose would Baal shut off the rains?

Zacharias: The ways of the gods are inscrutable.

Taavi: More so the ways of men who would decree
A fast today and proclaim temperance —
When flour is rare, the riverbeds bare —
To mollify their petulant idols.

Nasir: Peace now, friends, we are no longer alone;
Let us still our tongues, today grievance prone.
From outside, beyond our chart's furthest plot,
Comes neither man nor beast, but one besot,
Proved by matted fur on its wilted breast
And sun-scorched eyes that wildly express.
Who are you who enters this humble inn?
From what faraway place did you begin
To wander, it appears, fertile deserts,
This land of milk and honey redolent?

Elijah: From west of the Jordan to slake my thirst.

Taavi: You'll find no such thing since Tishrei beckoned
And Nisan, following his elder's lead,
Stopped up the dew proving that happiness
Does not flow from the riches of the sea.

Elijah: Happiness is the absence of sorrow?

Zacharias: Rather it's in the forgetting of it.
Now remember we have much to neglect.

Taavi: Those echoes are not yours, Inebriate,
But disturbed imaginings from hunger
And phantasms brought from sober debate.

Zacharias: I recall when good words of sound report
Would keep me on the edge of this fair seat —
Friendship din, tallow-lit, wealthy cask dipped;
When news of our King's good deeds would travel
Across variegated land, unabridged,
To land upon ears a concordant song.
Lo, not since before Baal has there been a
God within the temple walls to beseech,
Whose favors I would sacrifice to gain.
Oh, white dove! What lamb would I spare today?
Not to waste what drops of joy yet remain
Within this hollow cistern, I'll leave you.

Taavi: And I must return to the storehouse, though
The bundles be waifs and those to take, spent.
Slow, young man. Let me walk your tributes home.

Nasir: I cannot discern from your look the miles
Whether near, complimented by trials
That pay similar respects to myself,
Or from far, which so damages your health.
The light that accompanies you inside
Blinds enough the sense in me to decide:
If one from my own herd, apologies;
If a foreigner be, what policies
Have brought you to this desolate tavern?
What elixir must you seek to return?

Elijah: I seek no balm to heal this country's ills.
   I know where it will be found when time's seal
   Determines the fulfillment of God's grace.
   I come from high hills west of the Jordan.
   From the King's command to his vicious men
   To hunt me down — not just me, but all who
   Prove continued faith in our God — I fled.
   That martyred multitude, scorning release,
   Preferred a bright and firm resurrection
   Through flogging and jeers, even prison chains,
   Death from stones and sword, from spear and the beasts;
   They were consumed by fire and sawed in two
   In hopes of their disavowal of Yahweh.
   The world was not worthy of their yearning.
   Called by a voice like rushing waters, I
   Wander barren deserts and their mountains,
   Hiding in the hills and holes in the ground.
   Lonely and still, I doubted long and much
   Whether that voice be true, or I had zeal
   Too much, fraught with speech of my own invent.
   Then from a cave fed by raven's carnage
   And having drunk from the last of a brook
   The voice again like rushing rapids spoke
   Me to Sidon, to live in the Queen's land,
   With a widow and son in Zarephath,
   There to wait until the Lord's time has come
   And the thirst of our land will be undone.

Nasir: Were I now at my usual table
   Difficult to swallow would be your tale.
   But as I am clear of mind and sober —
   Seeing with one eye — I perceive an odor!
   Yahweh is now Israel's enemy;
   The age of Kings has brought its penalty:
   Our futures lie bawling on the altars,
   Little ones carried up toward their slaughter

So, Baal looks kindly on their investments
And any losses will be amended.
These fathers are sons of men long friendly
With pious rigors that treat them gently;
Their words lift a chorus of pure medley
Whose effect never fails to offend me.
Their tongues are like flames engulfing their own;
Hymns sung to divergent lords won't atone
For profligate service toward gods of horrors.
From heights of grand stature, they have brought her
To sordid quarters to boil small daughters;
I recommend this not last much longer.

Elijah: Yahweh has appointed His servant, Drought,
To return his children to faithfulness.
Would that repentance happen more quickly,
That the hearts of His people were softened
By the grotesque scenes they have seen and heard.
But I am not the arbiter of faith;
One's hardened heart is not plied by my hand.
I am just the vessel used to pour out
His indignation over faithless men:
Was I who called forth Drought from its chambers
And brought hell to earth that God may be found.

Nasir: I never thought to notice one so famed,
So willing to traffic in obscure names.
Tell me, what do rushing waters mimic?
What tone emits from the throat of critics?
Had I your instructions from such ill winds
Conscious alone would suffice to forbid
Raising hands in humble exhortation
To end the lives of this population.
Yet here is one for whom God so well known
He will listen for His word as His own.

Elijah: Peace to you. I was not so commanded
   To speak words that dried the land, but did so
   Of my own volition having seen the
   Dire straits of Israel's time: her rich land
   Was lush and verdant green, calves fattened and
   Coffers the same; her influence stretched to
   Nations far with whom treaties were arranged
   To the benefit of Yahweh's people.
   Golden ships carried tales of God's renown
   To world's end, brought back vile tales in return
   To sway the frail hearts of Israel's Kings:
   Belief in and mission for Baal. False god!
   Having seen I could not stand and so told
   The King with his Queen, the scourge of prophets;
   Having said so I could not stay, else Baal's
   Favor be ever etched in Judah's stones.
   When I return to my ancestor's land
   It will be with arms loaded for battle;
   Men must see to believe, or the tale hear.

Nasir: I am one without sliding loyalties —
   Neither agog at passing royalties
   Nor swayed by restructured societies —
   But certain gods that flaunt their cruelties
   Restrict adherents' willingness to serve,
   Whether it be Jacob's god in earnest
   Or the Phoenician Baal under orders.
   And I am one of these sincere mourners
   Acting ablutions in closet quarters
   Fearing to pass the way of all mortals.

Elijah: Take cover beneath my fiery tongue
   And know Salvation, permanent and staid,
   Will come whose shroud is long enough and wide
   To gather all who belong unto Him.
   This too shall pass, the rains will be again

And our Lord Yahweh will reign on high hills.
For if he did not summon me to speak
Before, He summons me now: rise and go.

3

ELIJAH MAKES HIS WAY north. Fed by the carrion of ravens he slumps through a harsh, dry land pummeled by intense heat. He takes refreshment where he can, longing for a hospitable refuge. Such a destination is less than favorable as the Word of God makes clear His chosen people are not to find succor from widows or the fatherless. Ummashtart is collecting sticks with which she intends to fix a fire and cook a last supper for her son. Elijah approaches.

Ummashtart: Out of the purview of the great god Baal
  We must be to suffer so, for we have
  Kindled our fires enough to consume our
  Bulls and guarantee the sumptuous rains.
  Has the palace retracted sacrifice?
  Have the sacred rites been neglected to
  Warrant the absence of divine kindness?
  Perhaps the King made Egyptian amends
  And found at last the means to irrigate
  The land, leaving us lesser worries to
  Keep tense eyes in sleep. More likely, if men
  Like gods be, then beguiled Asherah,
  Now concludes her marriage bed monstrous vile
  And will see the faithful starved to prove so.
  One year has passed since last the rain and from
  This land arise men like trees, thin and dry;
  Haggard limbs with drawn leaves that crumble so

And crack beneath a mother's brief caress.
Being already taut from youthful play
Deficiencies swarmed early to his build
So that a creator's architecture
Is revealed in my poor child — woe!
Fibrous muscles once taut, now moth-eaten;
Belly, skin-smoothed plump from retention, rashed.
Alas! Voiceless from painful swallowing
He lies asunder, dividing body
From spirit that is clawing its way home.
These sticks enough to ignite a final
Blaze and send you forth to a better rest
My son, my only son. May god help us.

Elijah: A long while through tortured scenes have I come
To the gates of Zarephath, besieged.
Oh, that torments confined to body be;
That wounds and lesions discomfit more the
Soles and palms, the brow and the back's tried discs
Then pangs of the heart that melts at such sights.
Yet still better are these than the ringing
In wearied ears: Yahweh's voice, persistent.
My words spoken in haste, true and ardent,
In tones inflected with visions of woe!
For my own succor I have called down death,
And that not merciful, being quick, but
Creeping patient through physiologies
Disrupting calm functions and processes
Lightly assumed in periods of peace.
Enraged I cut off from the land people
Dependent on her fertility to
Feed families and lift economies;
I have cut down my kin so to begin
Bracing times from great and powerful winds.
Because Israelites broke down your altars
And put your prophets to death with the sword

They have denied their covenant with You.
For this I have struck the first blow, rending
The temple's curtain that your face be shown.
Yet there are no armies assembled here;
Kings have not ventured forth upon the field.
Shields and spears do not litter the ground,
Which is barren of fare, even men's blood.
Still the trumpet has sounded loud — to arms!
The battle rages from men's hearts outward
Into the land: whom wilt thou serve today?
I will inquire of this raddled crone
Whether the spirit of Yahweh has come
Or if His terrible tolerance reigns.
Hello there and good day. I have traveled
From the Jordan's banks, dried now from misuse,
To come to Sidon, the land of your Queen.
Would you bring me a jar of water so
I might unstick my tongue and bring you fair?

Ummashtart: To you as well, though good days dissipate
  With the gods' good will. With it too our faith
  In one another, for simple kindness
  A miser, unless flesh be of your flesh.

Elijah: I am without family here and alone.

Ummashtart: And so now I must play the surrogate?
  Very well. A heathen's last endeavor.
  Remember me to god when all is said.

Elijah: I will do no such thing without knowing
  First from whose hand this home takes its blessings:
  From the altars and high hills of lord Baal
  Or from the ancient ways of Abraham,
  Whose sons work the fields and herds to this day.

Ummashtart: From the hand that is not closed, but open.

Elijah: From opened hands is His spirit released.
   Now bring me a piece of bread from your store.

Ummashtart: Man, as surely as the Lord your God lives
   I haven't bread, only a scant of flour
   In a jar, a little oil in a jug,
   And these stingy twigs, energy enough
   To give fire to our meal, my son and I,
   That we may eat of it, be full — and die.

Elijah: Peace, haggard wife. Go home; do as you say.
   But prepare for me first a cake of bread
   Then a generous portion for your child.
   The Lord God of Israel says to you:
   Your moldy flour will not come to an end,
   Neither will the oil's odor turn rancid
   Before the rains return to Yahweh's land.

Ummashtart: You have a strange way of speaking to me.
   Who is this Yahweh that we should serve him?
   And what would we gain by praying to him?
   It is Baal's bosom upon which heads rest.

Elijah: Then tell me: where is the orphan's donkey?
   Have they taken your ox away in pledge?
   It's a poor priesthood who forages food,
   Who combs the wasteland for children's cuisine;
   Lacking clothes, your sons spend the night naked,
   They have nothing to protect from the cold.
   The fatherless child is snatched from the breast;
   The infant poor is seized to pay a debt.
   Groans of the dying rise from the city;
   From the altars souls cry out for justice.
   Who is Baal that you are mindful of him?

Where are his storehouses from which you take
Your fill of fresh meat and vegetables?
Show me your cupboards; open your grimed drawers.
The wind is taken out of the bosom;
A flat salvation lies limp on your ribs.
I come lungs filled with a new Spirit's air;
Fresh winds will drive away arid beliefs
And return our Lord Yahweh to the land.

Ummashtart: If our fate does not take us in the night,
All you now say now I will do tomorrow.

Elijah: Gentle peace be upon you, dear woman.
While you may not be familiar with
Yahweh's being, most beautiful and true,
He sees you; He will not abandon you
To the emptiness of idol notions.
Ungleaned sheaves overlooked in fields are yours;
Yours the olives that remain on the tree.
The year of the tithe will remember you
Even if forgotten in the temple
Where the name of the Lord, when thought, is cursed;
Its rooms, reserved now for wretched business,
Once heard fervent prayers of sincere people —
They echo still in those halls of power,
Dormant so long, soon to awaken.
It was good for Israel's first Prophet
And Priest to bring the people to Temple,
There to make atonement for life ill-spent.
And in that holy presence dedicate
Anew her fidelity to Yahweh.
But now the Teachers of Israel have
Abandoned their Torah to mingle with
Foreign gods made of wood and lying gold.
They take too easily to wine and the
Altar's meat, demanding ever more from

A people already distressed from want.
Those better-born few of families bright,
Whose cleverness increases their wealth while
The voice of God and the breath of God roam
In darkness hovering over the sea,
Will be brought low to grovel in Baal's dust.
As it was before it shall be again,
For a tornado's wind blows through the land
And in its gale is heard the call for light.
From the gloaming of a wayward order
Arrives an independent prophecy,
Inspired not by befuddled visions
Neither influenced by Kings' policies,
But by direct revelation from God
Who won't leave His people unshepherded.
This mean divination will surely take
On the cause of obvious suffering
To bring Tyrian Baal and his circle —
Asherah his wife, Dagon the father,
Whose Philistines captured the covenant
Ark and carried it to Ashdod there to
Place over it the vile image of a
Virile apostasy; toppled at night,
Set upright again, to be found head-less,
Without hands and lying prostrate before
The Lord God, Yahweh of vindictive fame —
To task for the beliefs of this nation
So intwined with God's chosen, Israel,
Who have thrown off God's altar, brutal yoke!
If Baal be the bringer of heavy rains,
If exalted for lush yields at harvest,
Then I will shut off from his land the cause
Of his renown and grind his soothsayers,
Those nimble prophets, into buried dust.

Ummashtart: Very well. Take food from our cankered mouths
   To feed your starved dementia. But wait here
   While I prepare my son for good tidings.
   As if from the ground springs this deranged seer.
   When communal blessings dry up absurd
   Visages emerge from desert crags and
   From hills afar with ideas far-flung.
   Alas! what matter to me and my own
   Whether tomorrow we die or in three
   Days time? A crank in the wilderness will
   Hasten desire to have done with it all.
   I've found for us some mean sticks, dear child,
   But the fire they bring will not be for us.

Resheph: Then for whom does the flame crackle and spit?

Ummashtart: I met along the way a strange man who
   Beckoned me to feed him from our light store.

Resheph: And leave us a portion of earth and wind!
   Who is this man that we must starve double?

Ummashtart: Of god he claims, and he believes it's true.

Resheph: God has asked enough of us already.
   He has harvested what he did not sew
   And gathered what he did not plant or prune.
   Since I was able to walk, I have served
   At the temple as I have in the street.
   While boys ran foul antics in the playground
   And chased after one another's sexes,
   I was here, neither loafing nor shirking
   My duties hard-born from untimely death,
   Diligent in my ways and honor true.
   Yet here I lie wasting on my last bed
   With legs aching and arms starved of their strength.

Just becoming! Robbed of being's delight!
Spared dispensation by a blind priesthood
That sees in this the will of Baal!

Ummashtart: Hush now son, and rest your temper awhile.
Mysterious ways are not understood
By wise men let alone outraged children.
There is something to this man. His black eyes
Harbor leaden gospels ably carried.

Resheph: And for this sacrifice we profit how?

Ummashtart: Your sour mood compels me not to say now.
Silly old woman you'll no doubt call me,
And right you'd be but for no other choice:
A replenished supply of flour and oil
Until he calls again for welcomed rain.

Resheph: Ho there and be damned! Our store for mystic
Promises! Haven't we enough of those
From temple rites and the King's wise measures?
If I could bend my knee or support this
Fragile frame I would deliver a small
Fist of bread direct to his faulty mouth.

Ummashtart: Strength you don't have is wasted on mere words.
I will prepare for him what we have and
By the grace of some omniscient being
Be saved from this harsh existence, either
With new store or else sweet oblivion,
There to remember no longer the spent
Years adding up to a hardened whimper.
My son! All you shall know of this life is
Terror and wasting. Not for you profuse
Possibility: mists of wind-swept seas.
Neither will time ever be but a curse,

The incessant scourge of continuance.
Not for you a forgetting spell, a patch
Of disregard in which to run and dance
As calves released from their pens or like deer
On the heights dumb to the hunter's arrow.
Here is your bread mine true prophet, please be!
Tear from it and be sated as you have
Ripped last breaths from these sunken chests, Amen.

Elijah: Hollow-eyed daughter, do not be afraid.
    The contest is not between yours and me,
    But of the rightful provider of Man.
    Who was there when earth's foundations were laid?
    Who marked its dimensions, who set footings?
    Who gives orders to the morning, to dawn
    That lights ever-bright a man's righteous path?
    Has Baal walked the recesses of the deep?
    Have his feet trod the heights of Damavand?
    Did he create the gates of patient death?
    Would Mot know of what he speaks were he asked?
    Could he show us where pure darkness resides?
    Does he know the address of holy light?
    Does Dagon pull behemoth on his hook
    Or know the whyfors of its sustenance,
    How leviathan thrives on deep morsels?
    Does he know why its calves are brought over
    And from where they are brought? Say so, he does!

Ummashtart: Mad aberrant, you know I cannot.

Elijah: All such things are the province of Yahweh
    Who spoke the light into outer darkness
    And fine form into a shapeless cosmos.
    For Him I have dissipated the land;
    His glory brought suffering to your door.
    But my God is just and he will provide

For those who take up his own prophet's cause.

Ummashtart: Come then. See what savory words have wrought.

4

AFTER A TIME, RESHEPH begins to warm to the strange man. Their conversations deepen and soon he becomes convinced by Elijah's words due to the miracle of flour and oil. Resheph begins to seek the love of Yahweh, but no sooner has he begun than he falls ill, presenting Elijah an opportunity to impose God's favor on a foreign land.

Resheph: Bread tastes sweeter from not knowing wherefore
    It continues, renewed by friendly hands;
    Perhaps the mystic agency you'd have
    Me believe the province of Lord Yahweh.

Elijah: It is from my God, who promised me your
    Reserve would stay until I summoned rain.

Resheph: Why have you brought devastation on us?
    The fire of your tongue burns not just the King.
    Its thirst is quenched not by royal cisterns
    Alone, but from common wells is sated.
    Not my will to serve the Temple's pleasure;
    Neither would I sell callous statuettes
    Depicting small lives devoured by Baal.
    Of Asherah's poles we did not debate,
    Neither were we consulted as to where
    But told — for the sake of the land, its grain

And wine, oil and cotton — to celebrate
The fertility goddess and adore
Her sensual rituals that bestow
On us abundant harvests, Baal's favor.

Elijah: And where has that favor gone, my smart boy?
    Or for this you performed Baal's rituals?
    You've tasted dead sacrifices, corpses,
    The remains of bulls, of calves . . . of infants
    Strong only to clench fragile fists, wail red
    Before the blade divides life from spirit.
    For the spent pleasures of ill-lit boudoirs,
    Led by licentious hands to perform trysts;
    For the cruel pleasure of your twisted gods
    These haggard shades, attenuated souls.
    And in temple halls, dark corridors and
    Hidden niches opening into your
    Sanctuary: colored Egyptian silks
    Perfumed with cinnamon, myrrh and sweet flag,
    Enough to welcome scores of proselytes
    Whose shrieks and moans shake the mystic lattice
    And awakens He Who Rides on the Clouds,
    Reminding him of his obligation
    To reward such behavior with the rains
    Long absent now, though not without effort.

Resheph: Not for this, I'm sure, though Baal does not sleep
    On his obligation toward his people.
    For many years I have served his temple;
    For many more mother worked the gardens
    Of righteous men, leaders of our nation,
    Inside the palace and out. She planted
    The vines and delivered the fruits, the yield
    Procured for the King's pleasure and for the
    Sustenance of the court, his retinue.
    Diseases have tried to dismantle it;

Invasive pests desired its young shoots
But with skill and knowledge she thwarted them
From wrecking manicured lawns and hedges,
The perfect symmetry of crafted wholes:
Rows of waving branches fanning rampant
Scents throughout the grounds, strange aromas to
Foreign noses unused to such sweetness.
Each in her own way have been turned back, quashed,
Uprooted, destroyed in cryptic manner
To the unlearned. But to the cadre
Of believers obliterated by
Rational adherence to cause, effect.
Much the same, it should be, with absent rains;
Though I balk at such rites' efficacy.

Elijah: Keep to yourself the laden bin and jar.
  See that none enters your attic chamber
  To add flour to the store, oil to the cask.
  Keep a careful eye on that gracious store,
  It is there you will see the hand of God.
  Such a small mystery to bring about
  The affections of those used to neglect.
  When has Baal lifted a holy finger?
  Where the evidence of his omniscience?
  Does he know the state of his sacred name?
  Can he see the vigorous attempts from
  Lovers' chambers to woo sublime favor?
  Tell me, how long before effect takes place;
  Will the cause produce tomorrow, perhaps?
  Maybe skies will open in a week's time?
  To what extent will his ambassadors
  Go to call attention to his judged scorn?
  Will Baal puncture heaven with a fist thrust,
  Finally, at the high priest's own behest?

Resheph: "Not for us the mystery of his time.

Only faithfulness is required to
Reap the rewards of his divine favor."
So, we've been taught to recite at Temple.

Elijah: The land will be emptied of praise and still
Your god will not have found his own good time.

Resheph: If you mean it is his will we perish
It will be with joyful song we do so;
If you mean our tongues will cease exalting
The Lord of the Heavens, rocks will cry out:
"The Temple stones will pour forth their speech for
Any and all who pause to hear good things."

Elijah: The Irresistible Pest will feast on
The paltry sacrifice of Baal's altar.
Its hushed stones will burn from Yahweh's glory,
Fire lit first in my love for His true word
Writ through the ages on tablets and scrolls,
Passed down through generations that His voice
Might echo and His deeds be remembered.
As a child I was drawn to those texts,
Rapt by the faith of heroes, my forebears:
Of Noah whose hammer and saw could not
Drown out the scorn and taunts of his neighbors —
Those fated to perish in the flood that
Washed away feeble temples of false gods;
Of Abraham, father of all nations,
Who left his warm home for a foreign land
Not knowing sons were there; his wife Sarah,
Who laughed at Yahweh's promise of children
Because she saw many suns and was past
Age, birthed Isaac who was tied to the stake
Then returned to Abraham as from death;
Of Moses who parted the Red Sea and
Led his people across dry land, drowning

Egypt's quick chariots and sharpened bronze.
Jericho's walls fell at Joshua's call
And Rahab was spared precise sword's piercing.
And what more shall I say? You've no patience
To hear about Gideon, Sampson or
Even David, the giant-killer and
Warrior Poet, Yahweh's righteous man.
Perhaps you know about today's faithful?
Maybe you've heard reports from the palace?
Of those tortured, flogged, in chains behind bars
Or put to death by stoning, sawed in two
For the anatomical sciences
Or beheaded for going about in
Goatskins, eating things that crawl on the ground?
Destitute and persecuted, living
Inside caves, in hill's crags, stored in earth's holes.
This world is not worthy of their spilled blood
Poured out for our faith and for those to come.

Resheph: I have heard such things and have seen them.
   Our Phoenician princess has brought Tophet
   To the land, which we didn't know or care
   Because the fortunes of the nation had
   Blinded us. It blinds still, though we suffer
   This persistent drought. Still altar fires burn.

Elijah: These detestable practices and more
   Have been conferred upon Israel that
   Yahweh's love might be displayed through power.
   Kings, even of old, having grown weary
   Of Jerusalem, embraced strange gods from
   Exotic realms and put asunder those
   Traditions practiced by their own people.
   They caressed the beliefs of unknown tribes
   And lied down with their gods, languid, sated,
   Not knowing a jealous husband's knock will

Thunder across the plains and ring throughout
Mountain passes, careening along routes
Forged to increase the land's capacity,
The same king's storehouses, his harem and
The pleasures of men who would be like gods.
Such a spiteful hand is more to be feared
Than a king surrounded by his army
Secure against revolt, a mighty beast
Strutting behind his high tower, immune
From the evils that befall him, save one:
A furious man refusing his bribe.
When He comes breathing conflagration and
Smoke rising from his nostrils, the seafloor
Will be exposed, earth's foundations laid bare.
Darkness will envelope His cause from which
Hailstones like rocks will overwhelm His grounds
And bolts of lightning, like arrows, will pierce
The proud philtrum, shot through a golden ring
For taking a new lover to his bed.
He pursues the king and overtakes him,
Crushing him so he will not rise again.
Like windblown dust is this king's legacy;
Like mud in the streets, so are his honors.
The king cries for help, but none will save him;
To his great gods, but they cannot answer.
So it will be that day of disaster
When Baal will be blinded, when his ears fail
And Yahweh urges his redeemed people.

Resheph: Would that I could recover my former
      Strengths and see that day with perfect vision!
      May that blessed day come soon to the land
      And wash away elder complacency,
      Those too tired to remember better ways.
      Given food enough and time, I will join
      You in your victory parade across

Lands once destitute, now alive with praise!
Tell me, oh wise one, where do you reside?
Where does one make his home that Yahweh speaks
To him and lifts a nation around him?

Elijah: I am from low Canaan, of Hittite blood,
   Though land not our own, no proper nation.
   We were lone wanderers and nomads free;
   Ever thinking of the next lush season,
   Of finding spots to graze, our children play.
   If the rains were sparse or the grass too brown,
   We pulled up stakes and made for fertile hills
   Beyond the next pass, always out of reach.
   Unlike these days were the days of my youth,
   Still difficult to bear and I was left:
   Abandoned to the cold winds and the wolves,
   Thin as thread, that roam these barren places;
   To Fortune's dictates, either good or ill,
   Their faceless forces without fed altars.
   There was none to clamp my cord, none to cut.
   Neither to water my head and rid me
   Of my mother's blood, wrap me in linens.
   There was none who had compassion for me.
   I was dropped in an open field, despised.
   Then He passed by and saw my misery.
   He saw me kicking in my mother's blood
   Crying out to the wind to carry me,
   To the wolves to make their opulent feast.
   Like a plant of that field, he made me live.
   He washed my fragile folds, dabbed my bruises
   With oils mixed with myrrh and nard taken from
   Alabaster boxes inlaid with gold,
   Sandalwood and glass, ivory and bone.
   He clothed me in purple robes, soft and warm,
   And shod my burned soles in costly leathers.
   In his kingdom were many houses and

In those houses were many rooms in which
His children lived and thrived. And I was one.
But as I grew older, I saw many
Were not happy with their patrimony.
I heard say he was a hard man, reaping
Where he did not sew his seed, gathering
His harvest where he did not scatter them.
They left in search of kings who ask fairly
Of their time and talents, rewarding those
Who profited his kingdom with renown.
I saw them lay down with fresh practices:
Trading labor for favors, adorning
Their bodies with silver bracelets, filling
Their bellies with fired morsels of swine,
Washing it down with gulps from jars of wine.
They swallowed whatever was put to them,
Without question, without hesitation,
And traded their birthright for sumptuous chains.
Detestable practices bring Yahweh
To the Storm God's doorstep, his ensign to
The Cloud Rider's bronze brazier, above which,
You've seen, are placed your nation's dear infants.
Outstretched hands, inanimate, welcome the
Fleshly squirms of frightened limbs cold, writhing
In anxious unawares, being taken.
From a warm embrace to jarring stone slabs
Where steely grimness raw-strokes the babe's neck,
Coddling its panicked screams, abortive
Speech to defective ears intent only
To the priest's solemn tones ensuring rain,
Promising Baal's faithfulness despite drought.
Even now and for the last two years your
Children have been laid upon that altar.
With more insistence they've been placed and burned.
Like leaves in the flames their limbs contract and
The blaze consumes the body until the

Gaping mouth seems to grin at her parents.
Dying with sardonic laughter to the
Drum beats of sadists, the playing of flutes:
Fine symphony for a murderous ploy.

Resheph: I have seen the terror you speak, Prophet,
  Too ghastly to recount. Still the heavens,
  In placid repose, refuse us its storm.

Elijah: Perhaps Baal's fees reflect adult surfeit.

Resheph: Would priests recommend such a policy
  They should be first to hang off from the spit.

Elijah: Your terms are just and quite equitable.
  Wine-dark blood shall flow from their screaming maws
  Until they are consumed in righteous flames
  Careening from above like saving rain.

Ummashtart: That's enough such talk from you two tonight;
  Enough to last your still long lifetime, Son.
  To bed with you now and sweet dreams, despite.
  I would prefer you kept horrific scenes
  From young imaginations, understand?
  Even if you are not convinced, our ways
  From old seers passed down from like to like,
  The same way you received beliefs in god.

Elijah: People like ours endure through common cause.
  With love for one's destined community
  Comes need that it thrives: children, earth, water.
  These are the features of a healthy tribe,
  A health that evades certain of your ilk.

Ummashtart: I suffer drought same as my neighbor does.

Elijah: And that with a son to bear the burdens.

Ummashtart: Have I welcomed you that I be condemned?

Elijah: It is Yahweh's will you be lifted up.

Ummashtart: We didn't choose, my poor husband and I.
    Our kind leaders offered a pool, one for
    Unfortunate families to better their
    Stations, one for rich families to keep theirs.
    Our child would be secured for us, they said.
    Our gift would be transferred so never the
    Two shall meet. But on that day, the day of
    Our sacrifice, the day our home plied Baal,
    We knew them: he bent-back and bowing and
    She shaking, biting fists, fighting loud cries
    Lest the priests withhold our purse from broke hands.
    I gave to priests what was not mine to give.
    I don't agree with all our ways, Stranger.
    I am up nights until after the fires
    Die out. When the echoes of drums and lyre
    Resonate only in my memory
    I sneak into his attic room and look
    At him. I watch that he takes breath and I
    Pray that he tosses and turns that I may
    Be assured his spirit wrestles within.
    I have thanked the gods such an order was
    Available and I have begged the gods
    To forgive my house taking advantage.
    And I believe they have. Merciful gods!

5

ELIJAH LEAVES EARLY IN the morning seeking solitude. He walks through the wasted land praying for the widow's son whose health is deteriorating from starvation.

Elijah: Through dead trees and dried springs is your word spread.
    It speaks across barren plains of caked earth,
    Into the boughs' dried sticks, it is whispered.
    Good news is carried on the heron's legs
    Your voice, to new-made islands in the stream,
    Thunders aloud to the remnants of faith.
    Long ago in time, but near to my mind,
    The Red Sea was split in two, dividing
    Upstream from down, making freed men from slaves.
    Clasped hands entered the miraculous sea,
    A prayerful pose disrupting the breakers
    Pushed back the very nature of the sea
    Drying the bed with fierce and holy breath.
    Like those Egyptians swallowed in the depths
    So will the mad priests of Baal be deluged
    With the fierce insistence of Yahweh's wrath.
    Yet my peace is disturbed by twisted calm.
    The fields, once alive with the pitched chatter
    And wild frolic of creatures large and small,
    Have evicted tenants for withered stalks;
    For these stale needles and dried shrubbery

The land forfeits its stirring vibration.
Dogs, once used by resolute shepherds to
Mind their herds in open fields and protect
Camp from marauding packs, roam empty towns,
Now wan scavengers of filth and debris
Left behind by weary hands, malnourished
For the tasks of hunting and gathering.
Neither are there gazelles on open plains
Or bounding over spice-laden mountains
To remind desiccated hearts of love;
Graceless youths stumble over smooth-straight paths:
Their agility sapped by ruthless gods
That suck adoration from fissured lips.
But by this rough tongue is Your name made known.
Holiness coming from the widow's home
Calls out to those languishing in the street;
Into the alleys and dives of the dead
Cries the voice of Yahweh, eager to save.
In this arid land, with future bleak from
Fructuous memories, there is but one
I lift up, the cherub's aspect of whom
Your lush spirit gives special allure.
His body fails him and his health dwindles,
Released from recesses in rushed torrents.
He lays on a mat unable to rise,
Needing support for the slightest effort.
Once a lithe figure carrying quick wit
And a pack of familial burdens;
Is now an indifferent shade withdrawing
Into a fairy tale where, by magic,
The table is spread with olives and meat
Brushed by the fires stoked by solid timbers;
With fruit from his rows, sewn and picked in the
Time allotted to it, eggplants and yams,
Red peppers and squash served in golden bowls,
He prepares a feast for his ancestors.

Energetic shouts echo in the town;
The countryside is live with ruckus play.
With the laughter and squeals of blissful youth
Follow kinetic shadows, bold flickers
Of mind-play — acceptable offering.
Alas! my staff's hand shall not be disturbed.
The evil done by adulterous kings
Trickles down to the hearts of these people,
Uncounted natives complicit in their
Malevolent brook of vile policies.
The fruit of such seeds must be harvested.
Look now! She who is approaching comes near.
From the strong gates of her husband's estate,
Numb seeming, physically stultified though
Refreshed anew every morning. Widow!
Come now Mother, what more ails your meek life?
Look, the day of your ransom is nigh when
He pays in kind for the deaths of His own.

Unmashtart: What do you have against me, man of God?
What is so special about my lot that
You single me out to spew gall upon?
How foolish to be taken with your cheap
Parlor tricks, enamored by meager flour
And oil enough to add to my hunger.
Have you come here only to remind me
Of my sin and watch my son waste away?
Then be rid of you, for it will never
Leave my mind now my precious son is dead!

Elijah: Your boy is at last gone? Take me to him.

Unmashtart: What more can you steal from my boy's cold mind?
What is left for you to cannibalize?
No longer does breath reside in his lungs,
Nor will come dynamism from his tongue;

Neither from his limbs will vigor stampede.
There he lies, inert, fallen from living
Planes, no longer bound by space and time, yet
Tied to dreaming laws, to rules known not through
Experience or dulled by verity,
But felt. So, when I woke it was with a
Vigorous spiral of marvelous hues
That I knew to be him, my son, before
Hidden, released to celestial spheres.
Perhaps you wish to take that from him, too?
Robbed of youthful zeal you'll leave his soul pale.
With such ghostly pallor he now enters
Mot's necropolis, mourned by none but me.

Elijah: Give me your son that I may prepare him.

Unmashtart: He is washed already and been perfumed.

Elijah: I will not wash him with pagan water —
Neither will pleasant scents cover death's own face —
But through my spirit, that you may believe
Yahweh will take back from him what is His.

Unmashtart: In upper rooms you will find his spirit.

Elijah: Does tragedy strike upon this woman
To whom you led me a fortnight ago?
Have you brought to her miraculous stores
Only to take her very son away?
Yahweh, let this boy's life return to him.
Look, Widow. He tends to your anguish by
Hearing my plea. See, your son is alive.

Unmashtart: Oh, my son, my son! Is this truly he?
From a world far removed from this, though just
A moment away, could he have returned?

Is this not maybe another's spirit?
Could such a long journey for one so young
Disrupt his natural inclinations?
Will kindness vanish from his eyes leaving
Dull stares of indifference or quiet rage?
Will his tongue forget the sweetness he spoke
And seize a foreign dialect — spiteful
Toward all that is just, good and beautiful —
Having seen the demise of all good things?
Will his open hands ball with force to strike,
Or his feet carry him toward wicked ends?

Resheph: Mother, from where I went, I have returned.
   Though who brought me back and why will be a
   Puzzle even after it is explained to me.
   If that one had knowledge of the After
   They could not but repent their hand's dim ways.
   Here, lying on this bare mat, I suffered
   Pangs of hunger, thirst that could not be quenched.
   There are no sounds in the fields, no songs from
   The tops of trees exploding with green leaves.
   We moved about with pain in our weak joints;
   The soles of our feet bled on plush carpets.
   Life was a long series of unpleasant
   Presents, never-ending until we died,
   Each in our own way, uniquely alone:
   We looked forward to nothing but that day.
   And I had my day. My suffering ceased.
   I remember that last ache of anguish,
   Mother, was for you, alive still to face
   These eternal days of barren harvests,
   Longing for your youth, days of endless joy
   You will never see again — so I thought.
   Suddenly my fear was stopped. Such a warmth
   Invaded my seething heart and bid tears
   Of relief, of triumph — of Holy Know.

I was overwhelmed by divine auras.
So, when I looked to see from where they came
I could find no right beginning or end
Except within me. To myself I was
Peculiar; I was not what I felt.
Then a cogent quickness took hold of me.
Not only did I race throughout the cosmos,
Passing through nebulous glows of Forming
And over surfaces of savage orbs,
Through curtains of fire, colors untitled;
But my mind easily grasped the import
Of my heading: I knew toward Whom I flew.
I sped with haste to finish my journey,
To see His rapturous face smile at me,
Welcoming me back into His good will.
Then I heard His voice within my spirit
Say: Return to where it was you came from;
Your time is not fulfilled and I have plans
For your witness, both now and what's to come.
I was released from ethereal flight
And awoke with residues from great heights
Still rampant in my ideas of life
Then landed back upon this threadbare mat
Clutched by the wiry frame of this strange seer.

Elijah: It is for you to see Yahweh's plan for
   His beloved Israel, whom He wills
   Not to leave well in the bosom of Baal.

Resheph: If what lingers in my spirit be a
   Portent of next day's will and testament,
   What an awful display of God's power
   Looms for those oblivious reprobates.

Unmashtart: Now I know that you are a man of God
   And Yahweh's word from your mouth is the truth.

Elijah: It will not be long before He speaks again.
This time of drought is nearing its end and
There will be rains upon the fields and plains.
Fertile stalks of plenty rise from dry sticks
And tongues fall from the roofs of blistered mouths;
Eyes see and hearts believe Yahweh rescued
The land, that he has heard your pleas and moved,
Rustling around the heavens for his
Lost cauldron of refreshment, not worried
By how much neglect it holds.

Unmashtart: On that day we will worship the Lord.

6

IN THE THIRD YEAR of the drought, Ahab's belief in the goodness of Baal is shaken. Jezebel has sensed her King's dismay, but all her attempts to encourage him have failed. Meanwhile, the Lord calls Elijah to confront King Ahab. As Elijah walks through the land, the prophet Obadiah recognizes him and reports all that Jezebel has done to Yahweh's prophets. Untroubled by the news, Elijah asks to be presented to the King.

Ahab: I waited patiently for your lord Baal;
   Three years I have longed for restoring rains.
   I have dreamt being stuck in mud and mire,
   Of being waylaid in a slimy pit
   With no firm places on which to endure,
   Only to be wakened by wails of want.
   A new song emerges in my spirit;
   A hymn of lament is taking its toll.
   What more can be done that has not been done?
   Where are the sacrifices yet untried?
   New rites must be found to thwart our demise.
   How many priests hide rituals from me
   That, were they performed, would let loose the rains?
   How long must children die on the altars
   And how many more in the streets, at home?
   So many and so often that the next
   Generation will be a trifling age.

Bring to my throne those pious priests of Baal
That I may inquire again their proud say.

Jezebel: What more can they tell, my Lord? What else state?
　　The private archives of Phoenician Kings
　　Give no more advice than what you have heard.
　　There exists no secret ceremony,
　　Neither is there a hidden liturgy
　　With which to turn the tide of Baal's favor.
　　Perhaps the King need look toward other means
　　Of veneration to affect acclaim.

Ahab: I will have none of your veiled speeches.
　　Commit to Fate what you will, but clearly,
　　And take for your trouble rewards in kind.

Jezebel: My Lord and King, I did not mean offense.
　　It is with dread I broach such things with thee.
　　Of rituals and rites, you have not erred;
　　In speech and appearance are regal airs.
　　Nations follow your lead with faithful steps
　　To temple antechambers. And even
　　Altars do not weary loyal spirits.
　　Now, in trepidation, I bow my head.
　　All your majestic duties have been praised —
　　From the expanse of our Eastern trade route
　　To the treaties with once fierce enemies
　　Not a tongue dares to disturb your wisdom —
　　Yet this one chamber lacks conviction still:
　　The King's heart wavers between two Lords.
　　That realm has not seen, nor does it fear, Baal.
　　It is that land He wants, that He holds dear,
　　That the King keeps locked away, unwilling
　　To lower bows and open the heavy gates,
　　To make vulnerable the King's treasures.
　　As a sign of good faith, a token of

Surrender, give me leave to harass the
Prophets of yahweh, to plague their frail lives.
Set your face against them in an overt
Act of confidence in Baal's providence.

Ahab: What more allowances shall one man make?
   Measures undreamt of, but Baal stays his hand?
   The birds of the air have said to me, and
   Those that slither on the ground have shown me
   All that your hands have found to do.
   There are none left who remembers that name;
   None alive who lifts their voice unto him.
   They have been scattered to the tempest's end,
   Where the gods cannot see they have been dropped.
   For there is no whirlwind like Jezebel,
   No fiercer storm than Ithobaal's daughter,
   Who puts to the rack opposing priests and
   Carries from their tongues reverence for Yahweh.
   So attuned to Baal's jealousy are you
   Who strikes down his tepid ambassadors:
   By sword and by spear, tossed into the pit;
   Through beasts of the field and those in the deep;
   Their skins blister and pop in hateful flames;
   With earth they choke and with water are drowned.
   The voice of their dissent has been muted,
   Their presence in streets and squares forgotten.
   You have appropriated their hovels
   You absorb their fields into your estate.
   Children taken have nourished the altars,
   The blood from Yahweh's line has been let out,
   And still your people ask, "Where is the Prince?"

Jezebel: You believe He rests in the underworld?
   You imagine our troubles elude Him?
   I am about His business, as you are,
   Great and noble King. We are His mouthpiece.

With spirits adapted to hear His voice,
With hands willing to perform His will and
Feet ready to carry us toward His ends,
We manifest His being among us.
To whom would you have me obey, my King?
Is it to you I bend, or to Lord Baal?

Ahab: For all your contortions there is one Lord,
And by Him I receive the Queen's pleasure.

Jezebel: All you say I did I have done, and more.
Three hundred prophets, yet one man I lack.
Find that rogue auger of Israel's woe
And feel Baal's face shine upon thee again.

Ahab: I have searched all the nations and kingdoms.
My servants have knocked on every closed door.
Whenever a king or tribal leader
Told me Elijah was not at home there
I made them swear to me on threat of death.
Surely, he rests with the old fathers now.

Jezebel: Or else one in your employ harbors him.
Summon your faithful administrator,
Obadiah. Perhaps he has a word
Concerning yaweh's last dedicant.

Ahab: My devoted governor. Long have I
Leaned on his words of wisdom and insight.
My father treasured his calming mien in
Troubled times; surely, he has words for me.
I remember the split season of Kings,
When Tibni and Father vied for the throne.
All of Israel was in a panic
As the pitched battles fought in fields and plains
Spilled inside the high walls of secured cities:

Neighbors relieved their stress in fraught torrents;
Shopkeeps bolted their doors against looters,
Men and women once loyal to their store.
All night I heard the screams, and come the day
I couldn't see what it had all been for.
Finally, my anxiety took me
Away from the stolid childhood I enjoyed.
Inconsolable, my father tossed me
Into the irate arms of palace guards
Who dragged me from the strange affairs of men
And left me to cry in woeful corners.
Who would encourage my faith in men's plans?
His voice found a way to caress my cheek;
He lifted my chin and embraced my hand.
He led me to rooms I had never seen
And explained the ways of war against men.
He told me the power of fear resides
In its mode of hiding in the unknown,
But if we are brave and can shine a light
Into the darkness, its lies become weak.
He told me about Israel's struggle,
About Father's role in the ordeal
And why it was important that he win.
I was only a child, but understood
One fear had been replaced by another.
Obadiah smiled and said, "Ahab,
We can pray to God against our known fears
And He will comfort us and fight for us.
If we truly profess a love for Him
He is faithful and just and will guide us
Toward His will for our lives in this strange world."
Those words comforted me then; they comfort
Me now. Obadiah, I seek counsel.

Obadiah: My Lord and King. How may I serve thee?

Ahab: The memory of that wretched nuisance
  Plagues my Queen's sleep; she still hears the knave's voice.
  From dusk to dawn it echoes in her thoughts
  Disturbing her strong faith in Dagon's son:
  Mighty Baal, sweet to the earth is his reign!
  Go once more into the land, overturn
  Every rock, illuminate every cave;
  No matter the size of the hole, fill it.
  Chop down the tall oaks on Mount Hermon and
  Leave no sanctuary for that bother.

Obadiah: I shall send troops to the ends of the earth.

Jezebel: My Lord, I await good news of the catch.
  Who is this man to denigrate his Queen?
  My evening rest has never been so sound
  And I am emboldened every morning,
  Refreshed in my charge against Baal's rivals.
  One question plagues my day: who is this man?
  In this essential task to secure Baal's
  Standing in this wasteland, filled with echoes
  Of admiration to Israel's god,
  He resorts to dubious advisors.
  They have no idea where such ones hide;
  Sites of solace are beyond their vision.
  Were I to lead this hunt – were I so asked –
  I would equip a legion of fighters,
  Warriors laden with furious arms
  And acute focus on the horizon,
  To march north into domains not their own.
  The natural devastation of land
  Carries no terror like that brought by man.
  While the sun relents from its daily scourge,
  The affliction from human will shall last
  Until the final Tomorrow, constant.
  Who could stand against this army's frenzy?

Against their blinding armor who could spar?
They would cut a locust's swath through the land,
Leveling mountains, grinding stones to dust
That dissipates with evening gusts of wind.
Where could that deceitful prophet hide then?
In whose home could he pilfer provisions?
Whose solvent home, indeed! Obadiah's
Ready acquiesce to the King's request
May seem a loyal subject's own duty,
But there is an eagerness to his bow.
I must extract his incentive, somehow.

Ahab: Bend your ear to my thoughts a minute more.
The search has been made many times over
And you've proven adept at your errand.
Waste no more time on fruitless commissions.
Instead, take what troops you will; go throughout
The land, to all the springs and valleys, that
We might find grass to keep the herds alive.
And if the man be found grazing there too,
Bring him to me that we may discuss things.

Obadiah: Should the land produce fruit, we will find it.
Men! Trudge again upon land weary from
Pain, from sorrows plenty and without end.
Dust disturbed underfoot settles again
On hopeless plains, petty motes no different
Beneath one sandal as the other and
These similar at the horizon line.
I recall these cracked clods, once a seabed
Where lived a vibrant, if fragile, venture:
Interrelationships of complex space;
Of water and light, the energy flow
From one organism to another,
Either for breeding or sustenance, to
Form unique bubbles of biotic parts.

Into these are set loose economies;
Whole systems of markets harmonizing
Toward the goal of preserving life and line:
The shipbuilders and net menders, those who
Craft the sails and produce the tar, who plane
The planks and navigate by countless stars.
All made possible from vegetation
Forging compounds favored by animals
That are favored by predators that men
Hunt and gather for their prosperity.
Yet what can man make of dust? With dead flecks
How will a body politic sustain?
From such disorder comes revolution.
Through upheaval are authorities changed;
Old gods are put to pasture through new faith.
Aha! I see one with whom I must speak.
Of figure wan, yet bearing vigorous,
From durable stock and single-minded,
Able to shut off the heavens until
Such a time as false gods be unveiled.
Stay! I will speak to this one of sightings,
Whether fertile or dry, from where he came.
Is it really you, my lord Elijah?

Elijah: Yes. Tell your master, 'Elijah is here.'

Obadiah: How have I wronged thee? In what way offend
   That you send me to Ahab, to my death?
   We have turned this land over — neighboring
   Lands have been troubled as well — seeking you.
   When you were not found the King demanded
   Oaths, on punishment of death. You had fled
   To world's end, vanished from men's conscious thoughts
   To where no material shall reside:
   Poof! Now you ask, 'Say Elijah is here?'
   Where will the Lord's Spirit carry you once

I have left? Surely my neck rests beneath
The blade if the King knows we have spoken.
And I have worshiped the Lord since my youth;
From my early days I have sought his face.
Has the news not spread? Have you not heard that
While the Queen killed the Lord's faithful prophets
I hid one hundred in two caves, fed them,
Cared for them, bore their sorrows in dark times?
'Elijah is here' will sound my death knell.

Elijah: I have not heard tell of your brave exploits.
　　　Were news of that freely traveling, your
　　　Neck would already have its severance.

Obadiah: By the Lord's grace do they remain hidden.
　　　Though what is to be told to mothers and
　　　Fathers whose beloved sons have fallen
　　　At the hands of our heretical Queen?
　　　Where is their grace? How is God's love revealed?
　　　Are songs of praise to be replaced by screams?
　　　Are the wails of righteous men now sacred?
　　　Does men's blood now absolve a nation's sins
　　　And will such wickedness be forgiven?
　　　I have seen men stripped naked and boiled;
　　　Heard firm nails hammered through marrow and bone.
　　　I have seen piles of men scattered in dirt
　　　After being hacked off, chopped bit by bit
　　　From the whole, sawed asunder by bright teeth
　　　Gleaming in the sun of gleeful soldiers.
　　　Lions have devoured and asps poisoned
　　　Countless men in arenas and barrels.
　　　Millstones tied to wrists and ankles have sunk
　　　Others to the bottom of the Red Sea.
　　　Fire has consumed more, licks of perverse love
　　　To appease sexualized deities.
　　　Men buried to their necks and stoned, trod on,

Pierced through, galloped over and crushed beneath
Gnashing wheels of her golden chariots.
Beheaded, disemboweled, drawn and quartered,
Noses sliced off, eyes gouged out, ears run through.
Piles of feet, mounds of hands, testaments to
The Queen's resolve, that dogs lick clean by day
And feast on at night beneath palace eyes.

Elijah: Do not lose heart now, not on my account.
   We are nearing the end of the drought, and
   With it, Baal's influence on Israel.
   I go now to the palace to challenge
   The priest's authority with Yahweh's Word.
   Like the days of Israel's first shepherd
   So today a mighty hand strikes the throne:
   Fiery drops of hail will fall from the sky
   Scalding the resolve of cowardly priests;
   It will lick at the feet of heretics
   Whose soles will spark and flutter as if in
   A macabre frolic, ineffectual.
   Blood will soak dried river beds; into parched
   Cisterns will grim ichor find its level.
   In the land's midst cries will beseech favor,
   But like the landing of flies and the suck
   Of lice, such pleas will be swatted away.
   Darkness will fall across the land fiercer
   Than sun-settings or the total eclipse.
   Instead, gloom will attack adherents' hearts
   When silence answers, when their prayers are spurned,
   Those priests in righteousness merely play act —
   As the Lord Almighty lives, whom I serve,
   Today I present myself to Ahab.

7

AHAB GOES INTO THE wilderness to meet with Elijah. A challenge
is presented to the King of Israel.

> Ahab: Mighty in their stride are nature's princes.
> The earth's sovereigns lead with stately bearing:
> The lion — what power in his haunches!
> Such elegant calm before the fierce raid! —
> Casts his glance across the desert plains and
> Finds in his world none from which to retreat.
> The rooster struts among his peers, cocksure
> And gallant, plumed in regal quills, orange
> Fire and honey, of blood and azure fine,
> Assured in his place with hens and rivals.
> Curious and solitary, the goat
> Climbs over ragged cliffs, fearless of heights
> Where the air is thin; dominated tiers
> Of lesser bucks sulk on level ground, worn.
> Then the King surrounded by his army:
> On parade, through city streets united,
> March soldiers, generals, men of renown
> Who earned their scars and doled out worse offense;
> A string of horses bedecked in royal
> Attire, fitted in select leather bits,
> Carry golden chariots, sun-blinding;
> With wicked intent they roll toward grave fame.

Who dares to contend with one such as I?
Against a multitude of arms, who tries?
I am safe within their ranks. Fine-edged bronze
Expertly cuts down all who would oppose
His wise edicts, the customs he enacts.
Thus is peace certain in the just kingdom.
All of this is true yet here I am, King
Over all the land, with my awful troop
To meet one man, alone, without fear of
My wrath or of the Queen's reputation
For cleaving men from their gods — stratagems'
Sage for uniting disparate peoples.
Yet lo! One exists to turn the tables:
A lizard hiding in cracked palace walls
Eluding capture by proficient hands
Is no less a bane than this weary pest.
And like the coney of little power,
So, this one bore into the rocks his home,
Surviving on the bark of cypress trees
And the nourishment of ferrous pebbles.
Yet, by my hands he will be bound and gagged,
And by my faith his pledge will be condemned.
The Queen shall have her head; upon silver
Platters I will arrange his limbs for fire.
I will break his staff over my dressed knee,
Against timeless rocks his rod will shatter.
From on high Baal will see my fealty
And let loose rains on His righteous people.
Lest I am so blind, or have forgotten
The apt appearance of a worthy man,
I see a showdown shuffling toward us:
A wastrel neglected in bleak wastelands.
Men! There approaches him we seek, mocking.
Is that you, you troubler of Israel?

Elijah: Am I a hard man, oh great king, my liege,

That you come against me with armed escort?

Ahab: Difficult to find; easy to put down.

Elijah: I have not made trouble for Israel,
    But you and your father's family have.
    You have abandoned the Lord's commands and
    Have led many generations astray —
    Those whom the Lord Yahweh set apart.
    Now, gather the people of Israel.
    Bring these to a meeting on Mount Carmel:
    Four hundred and fifty prophets of Baal,
    With four hundred prophets of Asherah
    Who eat at Jezebel's table; bring them,
    So, we may frankly discuss the future
    Of this land, whether Baal's designs hold sway
    Or if green buds emerge to praise Yahweh.

Ahab: For years I have searched for you. North to south.
    East to west. From the Great Sea to the Dead.
    Jerusalem was turned upside down and
    The hills were leveled, plains scoured for clues.
    Still, you eluded me. My best stalkers
    Failed to catch your scent. Where did you go, seer?
    Under which rock have you eked out your life?
    In what fetid puddle was your tongue laid?
    In my palace are many storerooms, filled.
    Throughout this land are barns stuffed with rich grain.
    My wells run deep; they will never go dry.
    See, my men are well-cared for, loud and strong.
    With hearty throats they call out from their ranks;
    Able brawn carries them to the battle.
    Their arms will not grow weary, their swords will
    Cut and slice as if wielded by gods.
    Even now you see their muscles twitch, keen
    To strike down whatever threat before them,

Whether a vast army assembled to
Demand their hearth and home, wives and children,
Or a singular cause: the stable grip
Of an agrarian economy
Made sure by its homage to Lord Baal, the
Rainbringer, son of Dagon, Prince of Grain
And Purveyor of Rites, fertile and lush.
Voluptuous in His gives, palatial
Is his home and all who worship his grace.
His priests are dressed in opulence; their acts
Impress deities foreign and at home
With their vigor and sensual insight.
The plains are laden with Asherah's kin.
Mountains tremble at the steps of Her sons;
At their breath they topple into the sea.
Where is your troupe, prophet of Israel?
You are meager entertainment for a
Company set on tasting rival blood.
I would as soon cut you down in this dust,
But a larger audience you desire,
And I will not be called unmerciful
By one who fails to grasp what mercy is.

Elijah: You are like one who sees a vineyard and
Cannot possess it through legal means or
Persuasion, so you invite the owner
To your table and surround him with rakes
Willing to say he has cursed Yahweh.
For this you would stone the man, take his land
And ably sleep with dreams of wine barrels.

Ahab: I believe the famine has touched your mind.

Elijah: You would come against one out of his head?
With spears and swords, you will prod and cajole
This wasted psychotic? With shields bronzed

To batter and bruise this unstable mind?
What in this desert did you come to see?
A lifeless reed swayed by arid winds or
Perhaps a man dressed in regal attire?
No, fine clothes are kept in king's palaces;
What doesn't crack is fed by hidden springs.
Instead, you come to have your way with God's
Prophet: one who takes from storm kings their rain,
Who raids the grain god's store with violence.
You have not forgotten the words I spoke
Three years past, nor have you dismissed their sway.
I recall your ashen face then as now,
Back on your heels despite your vast array.
I do not presume your fear is of me —
I am one whose body severs from soul
As quick as other prophets exampled;
My flesh burns, my lungs collapse, my blood flows
Alike that will to death revelers send —
But of my God, who stopped the heavens their
Rejuvenating showers, who kept the
Land from satisfying its wet quotient.

Ahab: Do not mistake my pale visage for fear,
    But credit the doing to weariness
    And care for a large people settling
    The land after years of nomadic roam.
    Not for narrow shoulders this governance;
    Neither for a heart so hardened this rule.
    Wherefore this drought? Why now do the rains cease?
    Your primitive thoughts will claim god abides
    By whatever groans escape feral tongues;
    That deity is beholden to you
    Because you rattle the pan just so and
    Chant the liturgy with inflection clear
    To proclaim uncanny events. Naive!
    Look to the seasons then, you simple child.

Ever-true they arrive in their time. In
Cycles round, what was once will be again.
In my palace libraries there are stowed
Tomes, volumes of history and science,
Mathematics and astronomy that
Predict the skies so we can manage our
Economy through the use of archived
Logs of temperature, pressure, rainfall.
Thus, the King knows when to feast and ration,
When to invade and build up garrisons;
I can predict population surges
That will precipitate war and shortage.
Nothing conceals itself from apt minds.
I allow nothing to escape my sense,
But capture variables and forge ends
To benefit a compliant people.

Elijah: Your oracles predict observed causes.
What will be has yet to be seen by eyes,
Whether human or angel, let alone
Predicted through fallible rituals.
The King takes too lightly divine prospects,
He derides empyrean threats with ease.
"Neither dew nor rain except at my word,"
Yet you choose to believe in weather vanes
And rely on barometric pressures
Rather than believe the word of Yahweh.
Soon will be seen spectacles not believed
Unless one's own eyes behold the stark rout.

Ahab: Why delay until some uncertain date?
Don't defer justice upon fair nations
For trite reasons, but on merciful grounds
Call forth the rain from your dammed lakes and streams
High above, in the firmament gathered.
To me you came and threatened moisture stopped;

Now release for me the torrent's tethers
And claim victory over Omri's house.

Elijah: Your father did evil in Yahweh's eyes,
But your nasty ways have surpassed his gall.
Ahijah condemned Jeroboam's sin that
Abandoned Moses' law and led to the
Split of a nation between contenders.
He crafted two golden calves and refused
Jerusalem's temple her sacrifice;
He assigned strangers over high places,
Men from every people. No longer for
Levites positions as Israel's priests;
Religious service and education
Ripped from designated hands and given
To laymen without call or anointing.
You consider profane acts trivial,
Not hesitating to wed Ithobaal's
Daughter, the Sidonian Princess, or
Approve her purging of Yahweh's prophets.
Indeed, you now serve Baal and worship him.
You have built his temple and made poles for
His queen, Asherah — hag sensational!
You are worthy to rouse Yahweh's anger
More than any great King's act before you.
For this you will receive arrows unaimed,
Random assaults from faceless men, and fall
On the banks of the river Jordan, lost.

Ahab: You will now predict a King's common cup?
I would have thought you devised a worse fate.

Elijah: I propose something new: deeds to fire heed.
A contest! Let the people choose this day,
Whom they will serve, whether Baal or Yahweh.
Bring to Mount Carmel what I ask and in

That dust I will lie with my ancestors,
Or else his terrible face you will see.

Ahab: I would sooner have my men strike you down,
  But so that those remnants of Yahweh see
  What has become of their Holy Shepherd,
  I will wait for the silence of his voice
  To accompany your own tortured screams.

Elijah: There now, O Lord, has the man been issued
  Your challenge: will he praise the one true God?
  Early in the morning You found me; with
  My plow, alone, tending Gilead's hills
  You discovered Your terrible mouthpiece.
  "Speak this day to a fickle race these words:
  'Long have I waited for a faithful King
  To purify the Temple of idols;
  Its high places and Asherah's pillars.
  Prepare one who trusts in the Lord, Yahweh;
  Whose heart is moved by My word, devoted.
  Then will I return the dew in season;
  Plenty to your storehouses and cisterns,
  Vigor to the minds and limbs of Judah.
  I will be your God, you My people be.'"
  Forthwith I repaired to Ahab's palace,
  There announced to the King Your glad favor
  Would he renounce his wives and their false gods.
  Directly provoked, the King took offense.
  He spat me down and cursed my line and fields;
  He swore an oath my father would be killed,
  My mother lost in home's devastation:
  Wasting from want, cursing God, sorrow-stroked.
  I feared for life. I hiked my robes and ran
  Through palace halls, passed treasures looted and
  Vain ornaments adorned with the Queen's whims.
  Through the confounded arms of palace guards

I escaped into sunlight and fresh air,
But with the Queen's cackles hot on my heals.
She has taken revenge upon Your Word;
With the blood of saints, she has sated Baal.
Upon tomorrow's mount, unleash fury!
With nails spit, annihilate the priests.
Then the people will see and know Yahweh —
The Lord God of Israel, Omniscient
Creator of what is seen and believed —
Has dominion over the firmament.

8

AHAB HAS SENT WORD throughout Israel for all to attend the contest with Elijah's God. He has scheduled the prophets of Baal and Asherah to gather at Mount Carmel. The night before the contest he confesses his doubts in the priests of Baal, but is heartened by Jezebel, who sees in this showdown an opportunity for her father's alliance with Israel to reap great rewards.

Jezebel: The King's bed is a sorrowful affair
  Made feeble by a manic irritant;
  My influence in matter's grand undone
  By a soothsayer's profligate remarks.
  Throughout the kingdom reigns homogeneous
  Ideas of love and land inspired
  By the victory of Canaan's god, Baal,
  Over and above treacherous yahweh
  Whose prophets' tongues are now quieted and
  Whose hands rise in adoration of him.
  Unknown to the world, my replicate hand
  Announces to the King's subjects my will;
  Papyrus carried to the kingdom's end
  Bears upon its face decisions cast from
  Feminine wiles, as suitable to rule
  As any man's hesitant display of
  Kingly scepter withdrawn into the folds
  Of royal cowls, unable to flaunt.

Were I to brandish such a lord's symbol
I would not vacillate between two poles
But charge straight at one, outflank another,
And so, clutch one, destroying my rival.
Without gripping the shaft between fingers
Slender and fine, I made my lord master
Of his lands and over these, made their King.
How comes peace to these fertile plains? Wherefore
Glorious harmony of believers?
Not before my hands laid upon these lands
Could such symphonies be heard from or thought.
Disparate minds knocked wish against whim
Proposing works too far afield for
Agrarian faculties to consume.
Machinations of autonomous states
Form complexities interwoven to
Appear as few simple strands of cunning.
But we of quick mind and of artful plans
See through curious webs our own interests.
Would the king return to his marriage bed,
I would console fevered dreams — ideas
Of divine retribution stroked away.
But if he stays away, more time to my
Designs give thought and in their plentitude:
Sever the head of monotheism.
But no time for dreams of clever women.
Alas! returns the King to tire my thoughts.

Ahab: Tomorrow's prospects stir a restless mind.
　　For too long the land has gone without rain.
　　Coincidences besmirch tried methods;
　　Causal facts: useless against divine say.
　　Top men assured me drought was far off; field
　　Experts are amazed by the seer's timing.
　　Do mad men's ravings persist in the truth?
　　Do warnings of the touched inspire dread?

And yet I am afraid of the sun's face.
Tomorrow's glories are never secured.

Jezebel: What infallible sign do you require?
   Where is faith if you rely upon facts
   To overtake the hearts and minds of a
   Subjugated people already yoked?
   I will give signs; three of them I offer:
   Upon the hill of Samaria sits
   A Temple of such beauty whose purpose
   It is to collect the adoration
   Of a nation toward Baal, the one true God.
   Its entrance is marked by two stone pillars
   That rise to the heavens like strong towers.
   The space is lit by golden flames that bounce
   Off bronze basins and rattles; the altar
   Is overlaid with gold and draped with fine
   Purple silks fashioned by your fair maidens,
   One of many skilled trades to serve Baal, who
   Sits on his throne in tandem with the King.
   Lining the broad room are stele of stone
   Inscribed with depictions of your many
   Victories over those disparate tribes
   Who now worship our pantheon of gods.
   You've also set poles on the high places;
   On hills across the land are Asherah's
   Totems, both natural and man-made, where
   Magic practices are performed so that
   Baal's consort see displayed what we desire:
   Robust crops, ample rain, healthy children.
   Who would interfere with noble customs?
   Against such practices who would contend?
   That scrappy tribe from the north, whose people
   Cling to the bald idea of one god!
   Their temple is proved ineffectual;
   Their priests you have quit and their prophets I

Have rendered deaf, dumb and blind, unable
To influence divine acts or human.
Were their god true, would he accept all this?
Were he powerful and able to speak
Rain into falling or wombs conceiving,
Would he not grow up for himself people
Mighty to thwart the designs of pagans?
Surely, we are right abominations!
Upon this holy land: curses and crimes!
And yet who is this Yahweh? Where is the
One true god to save his people from our
Sacred sacraments and just reprisals?
He sinks to the bottom of the three seas.
He burns in the flames of our holy fires.
He breaths the dust of the earth, sniveling.

Ahab: Were the crown resting upon your head, I
    Would be so loose with my tongue as you are.
    Had I only to advise and defame
    Far afield from combat arenas, then
    Strong words of scorn and abuse you would hear.
    How brave to insult behind sturdy walls!
    Sure of an outcome is one without part.

Jezebel: Is your spine so bent, great King? Do cold chills
    Run ceaseless throughout your nervous system?
    Had I known you blind to kingdom's rule, then
    To a shrewd manservant I would betroth.
    From my own nation state are heroes grand,
    Of bearing and stature fit to lead men
    Whose ears would bend to my affecting words.
    Glory and renown to Phoenicia!

Ahab: Ears bend still, as yours to treacherous lips.
    Far from my agenda are your tactics,
    Fair Jezebel. Would that I knew your mind:

If only to see gears revolve for good
And observe benevolent arms that wrest
Their cranks, inspiring Israel's speed.
Three years since my friend laid his sons to rest.
Three years since I had peace without his words
Screaming me to sleep, leering in my dreams.
Those burial clothes. Forms laid in dark caves.
Mourned for a time now forgotten by men
Who take sustenance from that proud city.
Not since the day before she fell to horns
Has Jericho thrived; since Joshua: reigned.
And who cares for the lament of Hiel?
He spoke of these things and wondered aloud
Whether our steps had erred in their approach.

Jezebel: A people with faith in one god alone
    Are rigid, tempestuous and liable
    To march further into lands not their own
    And bring to happy tribes a holocaust
    Of slaughter and destruction yet unseen.
    I have read your histories; you have told
    Stories of forefathers: how they trumpet
    The close collapse of fortified walls and
    Wipe out armies of uncircumcised men;
    How birthrights are stolen and brothers rage
    Against one more favored in fields and herds.
    Ridiculous myths of a jealous tribe!
    Yet if by such ways they accost their own,
    How much more so their god against others?
    Much better the ways of Dagon's own son;
    More tolerant Asherah's espoused, Baal.

Ahab: What you say seems right, and feeble the hand
    Divine that sees rule thwarted time again.
    But while you remained at Abiram's wake,
    While you consoled Segub's weeping mother,

I was affronted by a man without
Fear of my right arm, wild with prophecy
Against my reign, my Queen and our true gods.
I have not seen one so raving and sure;
One who combines madness with reason sound.
His lips dripped vengeance as though taken then,
And his eyes burned holes through all they took in.
From that day the rain has neglected us;
Since last his words echoed in the halls, drought.
Comes this withered maniac to my door
To issue a summons across the land:
To Mount Carmel assemble priests and King
And know whose god be true: Baal or Yahweh.

Jezebel: Charging lunatics unsettle all men,
But don't mistake drivel for sacred tongue.

Ahab: Am I so frail of manner to display
Fearful cast? The words of men beget wind.
And such will his be, forgotten in time
Amidst dust and debris, lost in jet streams.
Alas! I carry them with me today.
I cannot forget augury's cadence;
The tenor of omens turns warm blood cold.
"Oh, wicked man! The sins of Jeroboam
Nestle close to your heart. Around your hearth
They find rest, and in their practice, glory.
Need the evil done be recounted here?
You know well which of the laws you befoul.
With glee and spousal assent, you corrupt
God's chosen people, led astray by wolves.
For the pleasure of wood, for gold's glee — Baal.
Embodiment of a usurping state
Who needs tribes eradicated to rule,
Whose domain requires subservience
Over defiant traits of vagrant bands.

As the Lord, the God of Israel, lives —
Neither dew nor rain in the next three years.
And this will be a sign unto your sense:
Chariots will not outrun God's favored."
The time has been fulfilled; three years have passed.
Tomorrow on Mount Carmel sloped with caves —
The haunt of criminals, abode of fiends
And refuge for any escaping God —
The ghastly day of the Lord is at hand!

Jezebel: I care not for mad hallucinations;
    The fever dreams of unhinged souls, I mock.
    Upon the seared peak of scrubby woodlands
    Our priests will gather; arrayed in gold and
    Flowing robes, they will position themselves
    At the feet of Baal, to his people true.
    Whatever challenge evoked from cracked lips,
    We will see the might of Phoenician lore.
    Let me speak to you the future I see;
    Allow me this chance to prognosticate:
    Shipping lanes and trade routes shoot out from Tyre,
    From Sidon pour great armies of the Levant
    Overwhelming the region with King's might.
    A world economy at our doorstep;
    Innumerable bodies clothed in silks.
    Nations will present on silver platters
    Their wealth and protection of our rich ports.
    Because of our guiding hands, the region
    Will burst with tracts of precious metals made
    Available through ceding us power
    And influence, extending our culture
    To the shores of faraway lands, savage.
    Upon the throne of this boundless kingdom
    Sits the Lord of Israel, Baal's chosen
    Vassal: omniscient, just and secure with
    Helpmate strong, able to impress sound ways

Into the King's ear, redolent of sage,
Of wine dark and joyous hallelujahs.
Such are the delights I proclaim to you,
That await hardy hands able to seize.

Ahab: From dire thoughts to cheer, you settle my mind.
    With visions of victory's opulence
    From agrarian economy to
    One of trade, you calm the tempest of doubt.
    Comes high the sun, on that hill will be the
    Last of a troubling people, withered
    By glorious suns and bright tomorrows.

9

THE MORNING OF THE contest arrives. All of Israel is present. The King's priests and army are assembled and ready. The King and his Queen sit in the shade anticipating, with the arrival of Baal, the eradication of Yahweh's dispersed followers. Elijah surveys the ground.

Zacharias: What purpose finds us on this barren mount?
   For what reason herded together high?

Taavi: Herded? Only you, too fixed upon drink
   To ascend of your free will, dutiful.
   Saw you from where I worked tying my cart,
   Staggering — whether from cask's innards or
   The push and pull of soldier's strength — unknown;
   Though I think more from sharp bronze and the brunt
   Of shield halting steps ably to comply.

Zacharias: King's men think wise to coax obedience.
   I emerged from our hole to catch wherefore
   The upheaval I heard, like thunder, from
   Across the land. And though the sun crawls high
   Upon its chosen path, my mind — thus tricked —
   Thought of a morning's barrage from past days.

Taavi: I heard the racket as well, but being
   Of sober mind I went to the window
   And saw the gathering force of sandstorms
   From three corners of King Ahab's domain.
   I hurried myself to the supply cart
   And made for the clearest horizon south.
   In haste I nearly ran this man over;
   Instead, I lifted his sodden gullet
   Into the tow from which we arrived, stale.

Nasir: I heard the dire call for all to attend
   Today's urgent forum, set to begin.
   My household packed what provisions we could
   Then passed through harsh grounds — though how we endured.
   Yet to be absent I feel chilled to regret
   And pray these jaded eyes won't soon forget:
   Look across the sands. Scenes not trivial —
   Recall the Gathering of Israel!
   Set before us life and prosperity,
   Or death ending chance for posterity.

Zacharias: Only one kingdom, the House of Omri,
   Do I see represented in the crowd.
   One congregation floods the arena.

Taavi: I have not brought in as many harvests
   As you, neither has my mind been filled with
   As many tales of our ancient fathers.
   When were such numbers foisted together?
   What were the circumstances that brought them
   To the foot of important decisions
   That impact future renderings of faith?
   Perhaps there is something that can be gleaned
   From this inexplicably frightful scene.

Nasir: Not since the days of Moses, frightful sure —

His chosen people to firmly endure —
When father's God brought forth the commandments
Upon the plains of this teeming land, but
With the slaughter of sinful Golden Calf
Three thousand perished in virtuous wrath.
The Lord appeared above tents in a cloud
Professing death for belief in foreign gods;
For tasks not difficult for us to laud,
Though knowing beforehand, we are so flawed.

Taavi: Then why this call to arms? Who charges Baal?
    Such despotic parades when none accuse?
    The Northern Army encamps the far slope,
    The near is held by Southern forces, squeezed.
    Their bronze and gold blind like another sun
    Come to ensure water's certain retreat.
    A company of purple priests: doe-eyed
    And pale-fleshed, they keep themselves away from
    The nation's stench; from street-strewn corpses freed.
    Lo! Another company well-fed with
    Bellies bloated from beshadowed cisterns
    Come to pry from cramping hands one more piece —
    A stiff price indeed for meager returns —
    Of household's wage to incite Baal's esteem.

Nasir: One man makes the charge, strong and courageous —
    Like Joshua, son of Nun, most famous
    For routing his foes behind and before,
    Toppling cities with unspeakable gore.
    This land needs a hero to stand against
    This land and their faith, no longer possessed
    By holy men sure in standing with God;
    Righteous men in this land no longer trod.
    Except one visitor upon our bough
    Who claimed nourishment coming in a rout.

Zacharias: Look! One from among the crowd strides forward,
    There to honor Ahab's emissary.

Taavi: I smell on your breath revelations gained!
    To conjure some poor ass out of caked earth,
    Have him forecast a battle for our souls
    Here arrayed in fine form; splendid trophies
    Worthy of any moneyed god's delight.

Nasir: The King's delegate seems insulted. How?
    Words spoken for select ears. Quiet now!
    The firebrand turns his attention to us,
    To make of this crowd his elect chorus.
    It's him. It's him! The brigand of consent!
    Listen, fair ears; strive to augur's intent.
    This is the man! His panegyric, our faith;
    Here to make against unjust Baal our case.
    Never again shall we suffer from storms
    Of dry sands and thick tongues. Our hearts transformed!

Elijah: How long will you waver between two minds?
    If Yahweh is the Lord, then follow him,
    But if Baal is god, pursue his leading.

Zacharias: What's happening? What did he say? Tell me,
    Why are we standing like dumb animals
    Staring at the mouth of a yapping child?

Taavi: He leads us into a choice most unkind:
    Between god that is not and one that jilts.

Nasir: I never heard so many so silent
    At the challenge of one to a tyrant.
    Was him brought the drought, an act not aimless,
    But he stopped the rain to prove Baal baseless
    And show the King only Yahweh commands

Phenomenon in both nature and man.
It is for this purpose we gather, flung
To this arena through fiery tongues
Loosed by a zealous spirit for our God;
Our love in return called forth to prod.

Elijah: I alone remain of Yahweh's prophets;
　　Whose head remains fixed, whose tongue to thought tied.
　　Baal has four hundred and fifty mad priests —
　　So great and varied must his demands be —
　　Who bicker amongst themselves who is best.
　　In rooms laden with lush spoils they argue
　　And with quenched thirst they laud Baal's faithfulness.
　　As if for them alone God's will defers.
　　For whose gain the captured blood of children?
　　For whose benefit the virtue of wives
　　When parched wombs cry out for wild potency
　　And cherished blood sates not this thin beast's thirst?
　　Enough sacrificing God's gifts to man!
　　To hell belong corrupt practices, vile!
　　Disparaging precious boons proves futile
　　For establishing the favor of rains.
　　Bring instead to profane altars two bulls.
　　Let the priests of Baal choose one for themselves.
　　Let them butcher and place it on the wood,
　　But do not set fire to the offering.
　　Call on your fetish, I will call Yahweh:
　　The God who answers by fire — He is Lord.

Hannibal: There is no argument from Baal's chosen
　　Priest; who satisfies Him is not in doubt.
　　Look upon my robes, my golden fingers;
　　There is no one fit to strap my sandals,
　　To wrap fine leather about honored feet
　　Blessed to carry Baal's gifts to his people.
　　For as many years as I have gray hair

My presence at temple has been assured.
Up through the ranks and deeper than my peers
Is my knowledge of Baal's works and favors.
I have seen sights to make you wonder, signs
That, were you to consider them, would boil
Your mind and make your tongue a bubbling brook.
I have seen numerous droughts, fields so dry
They depleted our stores and treasury;
They threatened my people's existence and
Brought foreign invaders to our borders:
Amorites from the east, like strong towers,
We overwhelmed, sending back as fleas, men.
Hivites infiltrated our seasoned ranks
But were dispelled when Baal's oracles warned.
Those we took for our own are gathered here,
Destined to carry temple wood and gifts
For the rites of a conquering nation.
And Hamathites from the north attempted
What your priests and prophets hoped to achieve:
Through sinister means reduce deities
To dumb idols and destroy the blest Host.
They even had a minor prophet who
Challenged Almighty Baal to a contest
And do you know what happened on that day?
Do you know what becomes of foolish seers?
Surely you must know. Tell me your slight truth
Or has the light of augury been snuffed?
Since your special gift seems to have vanished,
I present to failing eyes your future.

Elijah: Enough stalling, you decorated stooge!
Choose a bull and prepare your offering.

Hannibal: Lead to the altar this most precious beast
Lacking no flaws, neither in build or hue;
Perfect proportion his permanent horns,

Flush of high color pleasing to Baal's eye.
I sacrifice this blessed animal
In the hope it delights Thee, Rain-Bringer.

Chorus: Hear our supplication, Baal. Answer us!
    Your servants sing your praises, we shout to
    The heavens engorged with essential rains.
    Around Asherah's pole we sing and dance.
    May our actions today entreat good will!
    Favors like ripe fruit hang from ready stems
    Grown weak from blessing's weight. If You are pleased,
    Send Your conflagration. We ask for fire!

Hannibal: Oh Baal, Great Son of Dagon, hear our pleas.
    May liturgies like sweet music please You.
    Have mercy upon this worthy people;
    Give to Your children this one sign of strength.

Chorus: Upon cracked feet we perform leaps and spin.
    With aching joints, we contort our bodies.
    See our movements as honoring tokens;
    Accept our gestures and consume the gift.

Hannibal: Oh Baal, God of Fertility and Wind,
    Let our courtly alms remind Your promise.
    May what we present be pleasing to You
    And compel You to throw just lightning bolts;
    From Your high thrown send devouring flames
    And cleanse the land of wicked heretics.

Chorus: Answer us, Baal. Hear our supplication!
    May our music, made for Your parade, coax
    Your stark presence within our humble midst
    And show to this last prophet Your glory!

Elijah: How much longer this charade? Shout louder!

Watching this spectacle is punishment
For a crime whose evil is yet to be.
Do such exhibitions produce a rise
From your god? Does he enjoy such strange things?
If he does then maybe he is engaged
With duties pressing to his cosmic realm.
Perhaps he is traveling widths and breadths?
Surely, he has chores that take him away?
Or maybe he is sleeping. It is warm
And morning has passed; perhaps Asherah
Has sapped all his strength leaving impotence
Where vigor should raise its passionate head?
Voluptuous ambience is sludge-thick.
Put your back into the leaps! Those notes, mount!

Chorus: Though our legs be tired, our throats ragged horse,
We will not abandon these sacred rites.
Around this altar burdened with the weight
Of mighty beasts, we raise our hands to dark
Skies and cool winds, our palms await the storm:
Blest rains pouring Baal's kindness, abundant!

Hannibal: From morning new our ceremony wafts
Into the firmament, entering Your
Throne room adorned with laurels wide from gods
Unfit to be adored as Your equal.
Our voices emit warm notes of za'atar;
From the mouths of believers: sylvia,
Myrrh and cumin mixed in anointing oils.
Holy sacraments, for offering burned.
Now the sun lies heavy upon our necks;
The day has progressed with alarming rate.
Beasts rest prostrate beneath Your jealous gaze.
All the world awaits Your splendid entrance;
At the behest of righteous lovers, come!

Elijah: Good priest, he has seen this show many times.
   From ages past such frantic displays have
   Held his attentions, enchanted. Today
   However, he may have much on his mind.
   Distressing thoughts disturb his firm focus.
   Strange ideas mystify his reason.
   It is not your fault. How could you have known?
   When celestial courts are called away what
   Are meek men to do but wait their return?
   Perhaps he is returning even now?
   It is conceivable he has discerned
   Rotting meat in his nostrils, aromas
   Absurd to grace consecrated tables.
   I tremble to think what he will purpose
   From your pathetic display; whom he blames.

Hannibal: Double-quick time you poisonous prophets!
   Are your bodies growing weary? Has breath
   Quickened from disbelief? Do you doubt Baal?
   Turn now to desperate measures! Despair
   The efficacy of chants and spirals.
   Unsheathe your blades! Fine edges must taste the
   Faith of supplicants. This day requires blood!

Chorus: No longer for show these royal weapons.
   Baal calls us to a higher conviction.
   Remove proud vestments from deficient flesh!
   With hallowed knives run through unworthy praise;
   Scrape off foul arm and legs' meager presents.
   Let blood speak to blood our constant sentence.

Elijah: Of course! How sensible of you, great priest!
   Dagon's son wonders at your bizarre bid:
   How can a priesthood fat of arm and large
   Of thigh, with plump cheeks and joints well-nourished
   Beg for rain? "What kind of test this?" he asks.

But after he sees your bodies wracked and
All the gore at your swollen feet, surely
He will know your need and agree to aid.
I am giddy with excitement to see
His strong arm condescend to paltry force.

Hannibal: Louder, you fiends! Gash with bold conviction!
  Into meditation descend; prophets
  Of old revere remember rituals
  Long forgotten. Bring out from your secret
  Chambers rites unknown to we boisterous priests.

Elijah: Your knives don't seem to carry proper touch.
  Perhaps he appreciates sword and spear?
  Maybe the length of your cut is lacking,
  Or the depth of your gash appears shallow?
  Have you considered he has gone aside?
  Maybe your great god feels a pressing call
  Against his bladder that needs relieving?
  Perhaps his time in privy rooms lengthens?
  I heard some tell of such difficulties,
  Mere men of course, whose natures must deplete,
  But never would I think powerful gods
  Could be frustrated by hesitancy.
  Throw upon your altar fast stimulants!
  Mix with aloe, cascara; oil compounds
  May help feeble organs regain their roles.
  Load his cart with oats, rice and pitted fruits;
  Present to his lips jugs of clear water,
  Enough to induce such a bowel movement
  To encourage his wilting adherents!

Hannibal: You dare blaspheme against Phoenician Gods?
  When flames engulf this tired sacrifice you
  Will feel the burn of everlasting fire!
  Bring out the temple servants, those Hivite

Slaves to cut and gouge for new blood, fresh screams.
Assemble the male prostitutes! Send up
The women from the land to resemble
For Baal the purpose of our grand union.
Remember your contract with us, Lord Baal!
Rain Bringer, forget not our faithfulness!

Chorus: How long, Great Baal? Were we to sacrifice
Our lives for this contest, who would carry
Into future generations the rites
And liturgies of your Most Holy House?

Elijah: I see something coming fast from the west.
Rising up from the horizon: godsend!
Gouge deeper! Longer lacerations, hark!
The altar soaked in bloody prophecy
Beckons from afar your savior's notice.

Hannibal: Do not trust this fabulist's words, neither
Listen to his taunts; ignore his goading.
All that we can perform has been acted.
Our words ardently spoken have been heard.
Fear not! The blood spilt has not been in vain.
Ever-pleased with servants, Baal refuses.
Mysteries remain, for causes unknown,
Not to be revealed until a time
When we who gathered this day can accept
With honor and praise His all-wise absence.
Hold fast your faith in Baal! In Him rely!
The rains held back by His mighty hand shall
Remain entrusted behind the Great Wall.
No other god can wrest nature's control
From Baal's strong arm. Go on, you Troubler!
Lift your voice and reap the echo's reward.

Elijah: Your threats of death are as empty cisterns:
    Unable to manifest, I contemn.
    Listen to me now, you Israelites.
    Hear the word of Yahweh, the one true God!
    This day you will receive gracious embrace.
    Despite your evil turning to false gods —
    Your sacrifice of babes precious to Him
    And the infidelity of your hearts —
    Yahweh, rich in love and rife with mercy,
    Has seen your grief and now welcomes you home.
    All you assembled now, come here to me!
    The altar of the Lord, razed by vile hands,
    We will rebuild; with these twelve stones construct
    A shrine for the descendants of Jacob.
    Prepare for God's goodness: around this shrine
    Dig a trench wide enough and deep to catch
    The Lord's abundance, your store in heaven.
    Bring to our altar wood for sacrifice.
    With this knife, unadorned, for routine use,
    I divide the sacrifice and arrange
    The pieces for reprisal's consumption.
    Beside your altar our offering seems
    Indistinct; there is no stark difference, one
    To the next and with equal appearance.
    Your ludicrous prancing and garbled words —
    Your spend of blood to idols — I rebuke.
    Prepare yourselves for the day of the Lord.
    Lord! The God of Abraham, Isaac and —
    But hold a moment longer. He will wait.
    Priests of Baal, with your effective number,
    Take these large barrels to your reservoir.
    Fill these jugs with the water you find there
    And return them to this sanctified Mount.
    Be careful not to spill along the way.
    Now pour the water on the offering;
    Drench the wood in royal cistern's fluid.

Again, I say. Do it again, for Baal.
The odds must be bent more to his favor.
And a third time, if you please. Yes, until
The water runs down around the altar
And the deep trench has been evenly filled.

Zacharias: What is this racket that lifts me from sleep?
  Has something finally happened so soon?

Taavi: Never mind that, it was never going
  To be. He is merely delaying the
  Death that comes to one so disparaging.
  Look, the southern slope pulls back its arrows.

Elijah: Lord! The God of Abraham, Isaac and
  Israel reveal today that You are
  God and that I am Your servant and have
  Done and said all these things at Your leading.
  Answer me, Lord; answer so people here
  Will know that You alone are God. Amen!

Nasir: Wherefore this eerie peace? Why so quiet
  Now when before there were wails and laments?
  It is as though whatever breeze there was
  Has been inhaled from the land without cause.
  Even the wildlife on this barren hill
  Has hushed before impending riddle, stilled.
  Look! Darkened heavens now swirl and collide
  As Yahweh, God of Israel, replies.
  Forgive me my reluctance to believe
  And grant my family Your justice, reprieve.

Taavi: Is this too strange to be coincidence?
  Surely that man's words have conjured this doom.
  There he stands, erect. In the chaos, tall.
  And where is his rival? Baal's chief priest laid

Low, not in supplication true, rather
From anxious acolytes led astray and
Soldier's strength unleashed upon soft target.
It is a terrible thing to see grave
Ceremony expertly performed by
Worthy ecclesiastics turn hellscape,
Scattered hither and yon across this Mount
Eating whomsoever gets in their way.

Zacharias: Any attempt to flee a fool's errand.
　　In their confusion they have returned here,
　　Corralled by omnipotent hands, to the
　　Storm's center: the better to see His prey.
　　Look! Behind tumultuous skies alive
　　With furious clouds diving and screaming,
　　Like spirits released from hell's catacombs,
　　There appears an orange light. It throbs and
　　Bursts like the eyes of a jealous husband
　　When he sees his lover across the room.
　　No mercy shown when he takes his revenge;
　　However great the bribe, he will refuse.

Taavi: Great god of heaven; on sinners, mercy!

Nasir: The husband approaches. Provoked, he rises
　　To unleash madness: vengeance entices.
　　Bad omens assemble in skies entire,
　　Lofted eddies swirling in wind and fire.
　　This god — God of Abraham; Elijah's
　　God — has not been deaf to innocent cries.
　　Myriads of untold destructions are
　　Reminiscent of the famed donkey's jaw
　　Gathered here in this cauldron's righteous maw
　　Now returned to the line of Jeroboam.

Zacharias: What is this unholy apparition?

Pray god I remain in oblivion
And this be only a heinous mirage!

Taavi: You are Lord God of Abraham, Isaac —

Zacharias: Such dire events in the vast firmament!
Never has the sky been lit afire so.
Even upon the earth such glows unknown.
And what this! Molten whips of searing clouds
Drip from roiling thunderheads broken off
From the malicious storm front. Opening!
Solid mists, enflamed, lick their greedy lips.
Tongues of fire speak terrible words of woe.
And there! A column all ablaze and wound
With flak shooting off in all directions;

Taavi: People will know that You alone are God!

Nasir: The conflagration is at an end. Look!
Baal and his court no longer will be brooked.
Not only has the bull been accepted,
But the wood too has evaporated.
Bodies, once men, upon the charred filed strewn;
Their beliefs, like Asherah's poles, lie hewn.
Even the stones after the fire lie flattened,
Crushed by the flames, reduced to their atoms.
Those merely singed wail at the awesome sight
Of Yahweh's wrath direct from Heaven bright.

Taavi: The Lord — He is God! Yahweh, He is God!

Chorus: Had we not seen for ourselves, faithless be.
Surely Baal has been annihilated
By this fierce deity! At the hands of
Israel's God, hurled into an abyss.
The ethereal hell storm burned our eyes!

Better not to see each other's bodies
Flayed and speared; punctured, gashed, mangled and torn.
Our bodies have spared no inch, not a stretch
Remains that haven't been offered to Baal.
Take for your god, Yahweh who Saves, the rest.

Zacharias: One prophet steps forth from the charred carnage.

Elijah: Seize Baal's prophets. Whoever has survived
Yahweh's quick wrath will be taken away
To the Kishon Valley and slaughtered there.
Tell Ahab, 'Go, eat and drink, for there is
A sound of heavy rain.' But I will wait
Upon this mountain for God's cooling face.
Turn wherever I will, by night or day,
Either in seasons dry or in the storm,
Your Spirit beckons me turn and obey
Your dynamic word, a man to transform.
Yet when did my voice reason to imply
Strong arm's might against such troubled beliefs
To warrant bold smite turning all to grief?
I am leveled in dust that You replied.
Oh, God! Mighty to save and strong the same;
Hallowed be this ground like Your Holy Name.
Who stumbles there? Go and look toward the sea.

Nasir: There is nothing there to report, my lord;
Blue skies contrary to augur's reward.
Who is this who calls down softening fire
Upon heretic's retinue entire?
So shown the banality of their god,
They hold their foremost lives in disregard.
Without cause for celebration, he lies
Distraught seeming at enemy's demise;
All around him the sure route is at hand,
The blood of his foes stains then soaks the sand.

Elijah: I am tired from running; from hiding in
  The crags of rocks and hovels of the poor.
  Just let me sit here, face between my knees,
  And meditate on the good God has done.

Nasir: A cloud, small as a fist, comes from the sea!

Elijah: That will do, faithful servant. That will do.

10

Having defeated the religion of Baal, Elijah and his faithful servant take cover from the heavy rains. Obadiah seeks Elijah for conference.

Obadiah: How pleasant the sound of heavy droplets.
  Thick pellets of rain exploding ancient
  Dusts, washing away three years of absence,
  Brings to weary bones a peaceful repose.
  I have forgotten the feel of cool winds
  Against my cheek, walking through damp grasses
  And the joyful songs of nature's creatures
  Leaping from their stalls, dancing in puddles.
  No longer are the seasons in Baal's hands;
  Pray not to Canaan's gods for Yahweh's store.
  The God of Israel has taken that
  Province from foreign empires; from prophets
  Who see with calculated intentions
  He withholds truth and abundant honors.
  Where are those who proclaim the might of Baal?
  Who provides trumpet's breath and who lifts arms
  To defend the veracity of Baal?
  Their hearts have been stopped by miracles dire;
  Through marvels unheard of they have passed on.
  Even their bodies have returned to dust,
  Leaving no marker for heirs to visit.

Save one, I see, in the sand up ahead;
One solitary spire aloft on high.
But stay, my prayerful lips; restrain your joy
Until his temper has been determined
For fear I say wrong words and bring upon
His tongue further coals when cooling drinks need.

Nasir: Never have I thought, nor even suspect,
A slayer of men could be so direct.
Who would believe such a story as this?
Facts of the day against reason resists.
Would I had a tablet or papyrus
To regale future minds our happiness
At being justified through faith in God
And perceiving His outstretched hand, respond.
I will search the surrounds for noble stones
To raise a trusted altar to our Lord.

Elijah: Calm yourself. Yahweh's will has been fulfilled.
The blood of thousands calling from the ground
Has been silenced; vengeance has sated them.
There he flies, hunting for substantial stones
To commemorate upon this portion
Your faithfulness to unflinching servants.
Who am I that You would listen to words
Spoken in haste with impatience at heart?
On the run from regret, with doubt affixed,
You spoke comforting peace to pensive caves.
Ravens came to me direct from Your hand;
Despite cold nights, hope never left my breast.
How You have helped the powerless today!
How You have saved the arms that are feeble!
From deep anguish to revolt's joyful coup
The pendulum swing lays my spirit low.
Too quick and with much savage pageantry
Has the tide changed and left me overwhelmed.

Your goodness is too much for me to bear;
A moment more, let me lie here distressed —
Drained of all passion, Lord, grant me rest.

Nasir: It is good for me to be here, my lord,
To construct these altars for new abodes.
On this spot shall rise a people honest
And true in their worship, duly promised.
Though offerings meager in this dryness
Let us return to these stones three years hence
With appropriate gifts for savior's want
To rescue us, His ruinous deeds we vaunt.
I present myself for holy orders,
Difficult call, but worthy to shoulder.

Elijah: We are not without priests to serve the cause.
There remains a remnant hidden away
From Jezebel's hand, now pleased to reveal
Yahweh's word for people chosen again
To be His tribe to the ends of the earth.

Nasir: Would I could join their consecrated ranks
And be counted sacred. To you be thanks —
Alas! my blood does not follow that line;
At your word, patrimony reassigned . . .
But here comes one through the smoldering ash.
Another contender with whom to clash!
State your peaceful business or be run through
By sword unsheathed, your will to ours subdued;
Approach with contrition your sinful ways
And turn to righteousness, alone Yahweh's!

Obadiah: Greetings Elijah, Troubler of Baal!
Yahweh's great Prophet and Bane of Ahab,
Peace to you and your zealous companion.
I have been and always will be a friend.

The annals of Kings have not recorded
Sights to compare with what I saw today.
From the plains yonder I watched you approach,
Afraid that before you uttered a word,
King Ahab would have you struck down, clobbered
With sticks and stones, spears and the knife's sharp edge.
When you remained standing, Spirit within,
I thanked God for preserving your mean life.
Then what did I hear? I couldn't believe!
And still you remained standing, defiant.
Have the gods ever been so abused, so
Taunted and scorned that their priests and prophets
Abide blasphemies, that they be proved wrong?

Elijah: It is the nature of false gods to know
　Their place in the cosmic hierarchy.

Obadiah: Today you have wiped the presence of Baal
　From Yahweh's promised land to Israel.
　In years to come our children's children will
　Ask about and be reminded of this
　Faithful day, the day Yahweh's people ceased
　Being transients of wild leanings; with
　Spirit crude bestowed with relentless wills
　To survive the wiles of nature and her
　Serpent's cults. On this day, the day fire rained
　From heaven, Yahweh has made clear Baal is
　No peer of his preeminent judgment.
　There is not another God like our God,
　Who has rescued us from apostasies,
　Vile and numerous, that we stretched for and
　Grabbed with both hands, the better to succeed
　In foreign lands. Thanks to His great mercy,
　Elijah was sent to prepare the board:
　To assemble pieces and set the rules;
　To summon the challenge and win the pale

Hearts of Israel and Canaan alike.
From this day forward, Israel shall be
Like a chosen people again: a light
Unto the nations, exemplars of His
Covenant with mankind, we will advance
The truth of His divinity into
Faraway lands by our dealings with them;
Through our witness all the kingdoms of earth
Will surely hear the name of God. No more
Will we wait for foreign petitions,
But will rest in staid modesty before
The Lord God — Yahweh is His name. Amen.

Elijah: Without doubt, Yahweh has won this day's prize;
    With fire and storm called from provinces rare
    He established His reign in this land.
    Look across this charred earth and see: remnants
    Of a strong people well-clad; in arms, skilled;
    With relentless vigor in meaning, true.
    Yet, in all these ways were they led astray.
    Right does not come from might, nor from sharpened
    Bronze, but from faith in Yahweh's strong right arm
    And from His voice that utters no false word.
    The voice of the Lord covers the waters;
    It shakes the desert and strips forests bare.
    The Lord's voice strikes with flashes of lightning
    And breaks cedars of Lebanon in two.
    The Lord sits enthroned over Israel;
    Over His people does He rule supreme.
    In my despair over Israel's sins
    I cried out. From His temple He heard me.
    My lament reached his ears and roused Yahweh.
    The earth trembled and quaked, the mountains shook.
    He parted the clouds and leaned in to look.
    There before Him danced Baal's priests and prophets.
    In their ecstasy they failed to notice

The eyes of God were watching their pageant.
But their gestures were not for Him, neither
Were their words spoken in a tongue He knew.
They spilled blood that Yahweh did not demand;
What God requires they did not put forward.
Yahweh looked across space and time to find
This Baal that was being fervently called;
But there is none but Him. Yahweh alone is.
Smoke rose from His nostrils; consuming fire
Poured from His mouth and burning coals rained down.
He devoured the heretics where they stood.
Not one escaped from His fiery sentence
And from His temple we cry out, "Glory!"

Obadiah: So it was just as you had spoken it.
The healing rains have come at your command.

Nasir: There are some whom the Lord saw fit to spare.
I see King Ahab carried off in fear.
His fleet chariot flees, though none pursue,
Racing down Mount Carmel tossing up dew.
Why has the Lord given up the battle;
Have enemies regroup, restore mettle?
Will he triumph after all despite mad
Ravings of one assured, faith ironclad
In one show of strength, though convincing may be,
Forgetting three years of hope absentee?

Elijah: The King and his wife are soon to be mourned;
In the Lord Yahweh's good time they will die.
See, the heavens have opened in relief.
Refreshing rains fall on faithful heads and
Upon the earth green shoots will spread, verdant.
I had been shown all of this and foretold.
As many years ago that I foresaw
Are the years until the King's wounds end him.

Now I see the Lord sitting on His throne.
The hosts of Heaven surround His glory.
On His right are the legions of Michael
Bedecked in armor, draped in scarlet cloth,
The archangel wields high his fiery blade.
His blue eyes are keen, his focus is sharp
Upon the right task to which he is called.
Being Israel's advocate, he leads
The charge against the enemies of state.
White knuckles surround the hilt of his sword
Gripped tight as around the throats of our foes.
Gabriel kneels at Lord Yahweh's left hand.
Emerald robes belie his matchless strength.
In quiet contemplation he prepares
For the battle nigh, its outcome foreseen
Since before the earth from chaos was formed.
The Lord spoke across the heavenly hordes:
"Who will entice Ahab? Who will send him
To Ramoth Gilead and his death there?"
From within the ranks a noble spirit
Emerged, grand. "I will entice him to go."
"By what means?" To which the spirit replied:
"By deceiving augurs in prophets' mouths
He will attack the Amorites and fail."
To which the Lord: "Let your plan befall him.
In Ramoth Gilead he will drop from
Aramean arrows sped fast into
The gaps of his armor. They will bury
Him in Samaria; beside a pool
They will wash the gore from his chariot,
And dogs will lick his blood," declares Yahweh.

Obadiah: As the Lord decrees, so shall it be. Though
    The King turned from the faith of his father's
    And embraced the sins of Jeroboam, he
    Was anointed head of Yahweh's chosen.

On that day I led the worthy procession
To honor that divine consecration.
But what of his foreign bride, Jezebel?
Has the Lord shown you that woman's demise?

Elijah: She goes now to Jezreel, never to leave.
In her high tower she will manage the
King's affairs, consulting and advising
With emissaries and ambassadors
Until the time comes for her to expire.
Three eunuchs charged with the Queen's protection
Will adhere to the commands of Jehu,
King of Israel, exterminator
Of the annals of Ahab and his line.
Made up and arranged for effect, the Queen
Will welcome Jehu and his retinue.
"Who is on my side?" and with these words the
Eunuchs will grapple with proud Jezebel
And throw her from the high tower's refuge.
When the servants return to bury her
They will find only the skull, hands and feet.
Thus, will be fulfilled Yahweh's words to me:
"Dogs will ravage Jezebel in Jezreel."

Obadiah: May the Lord's words come to pass, and quickly.

Nasir: My lord, a staid messenger approaches.
Upon holy land this fiend encroaches!
What sayings from the King will you allow
Him to speak? Whatever truth, I disavow.
My sword has been thirsty since fire I saw
Pour down from Heaven bringing men to awe.
Give me this privilege: to protect God's own
From evil words persuasive, bad seeds sewn.
Give me the word and this blade will right feast
On the blood of this man disguised, a beast!

Elijah: Look upon this meager requite. Tell us
What threat beckons from such humble response?
Return proud sword to zealous scabbard fond.
Perhaps this good lord seeks favor not found
In the halls of Baal's temple recently
Raised power of faith in your Yahweh.
Come closer, poor man, and speak what you'll say;
What message has the King charged you today?

Messenger: From the King, nothing, but from Jezebel
I bring these words to lay at your bare feet:
My Queen has heard of today's poor defeat
And has issued me this missive, tell:
"May the gods deal with me, even gravely,
If by tomorrow your life is not mine.
You shall not rest, my heart's so inclined
To burden you with dread, far from safety.
I am ever so versed in torture fine
To bring zealous hearts to recant proud faith.
Poor spirits I find when their peers do bathe
In blood spilled loosely, their souls hoarded, mine.
So will be yours, mad seer of our demise,
I will echo your say while beg, 'Relent!'
And listen to words of life poorly spent."
Thus, the Queen's message, she calls you advise
This cloudy warning from she who speaks truth
Darker than your cloud, unable to sooth.

Elijah: As today's divine phenomenon showed,
There is no God but Israel's Yahweh.
Tell your Queen that I am safely His own;
If I am alive tomorrow, His say.
My life belongs to Him, highly favored;
More to reveal so long as I have breath
To speak His good will, life with Him savored,
Width to proclaim and still more sacred breadth.

Tell your Queen I await profaned sentence
And pray to God her life brings repentance.
Now leave us in peace to meditate cause,
Such are the ways of Yahweh, God of gods.